This book is to be returned on or before
the last date stamped below.

24. NOV. 1994

14. FEB. 1986

7. MAR. 1986

17 DEC 2015

21. MAR. 1986

29. NOV. 1989

-2 DEC 1993

Penguin Books
Children Are Civilians Too

Heinrich Böll was born in Cologne in 1917. The son of a
sculptor, he began work in a bookshop, then served in
the infantry throughout the war. After 1945 he took
various jobs, becoming a freelance writer in 1951. He
has since worked as a novelist, short-story writer and
radio playwright. His first novels, *The Train Was on
Time* and *And Where Were You, Adam?*, concerned the
despair of those involved in total war; his later works,
including *The Unguarded House*, deal with the moral
vacuum behind the post-war 'economic miracle' in
Western Germany, and *The Bread of Those Early Years*
depicts the poverty, the greyness and the continual
hunger of the period shortly after the war. In his short-
story writing Böll is regarded as one of the founders
of the contemporary German American-style *Kurz-
geschichte*. Among his other novels are *The End of a
Mission* (1968), *Group Portrait with Lady* (1973), *The
Lost Honour of Katharina Blum* (1975) and *The Safety
Net* (1982). Heinrich Böll was elected the first Neil Gunn
Fellow by the Scottish Arts Council in 1970 and was
awarded the Nobel Prize for Literature in 1972. He is
an outspoken defender of artistic freedom, a past
president of International PEN, and has been active
on behalf of Solzhenitsyn and other writers throughout
the world.

Heinrich Böll

Children Are Civilians Too

Translated from the German by
Leila Vennewitz

Penguin Books

Penguin Books Ltd, Harmondsworth, Middlesex, England
Penguin Books, 40 West 23rd Street, New York, New York 10010, U.S.A.
Penguin Books Australia Ltd, Ringwood, Victoria, Australia
Penguin Books Canada Ltd, 2801 John Street, Markham, Ontario, Canada L3R 1B4
Penguin Books (N.Z.) Ltd, 182–190 Wairau Road, Auckland 10, New Zealand

This translation first published in the U.S.A. 1970
Published in Great Britain by
Martin Secker & Warburg 1973
Published in Penguin Books 1976
Reprinted 1984

Made and printed in Singapore by
Richard Clay (S.E. Asia) Pte Ltd
Set in Monotype Plantin

Translator's Acknowledgement

My husband, William Vennewitz,
has assisted me greatly
in the translation of this book,
and I am deeply grateful to him.

Leila Vennewitz

These stories formed part of a volume entitled *1947 bis 1951*, published in German 1964.

Dates of original German publication of the stories are as follows: Across the Bridge – 1950; My Pal with the Long Hair – 1947; The Man with the Knives – 1948; Rise, My Love, Rise – 1950; That Time We Were in Odessa – 1950; 'Stranger, Bear Word to the Spartans We . . .' – 1950; Drinking in Petöcki – 1950; Dear Old Renée – 1950; Children Are Civilians, Too – 1950; What a Racket – 1950; At the Bridge – 1950; Parting – 1950; Breaking the News – 1947; Reunion with Drüng – 1950; The Ration Runners – 1950; Reunion in the Avenue – 1948; In the Darkness – 1950; Broommaker – 1950; My Expensive Leg – 1950; Lohengrin's Death – 1950; Business is Business – 1950; On the Hook – 1950; My Sad Face – 1950; Candles for the Madonna – 1950; Black Sheep – 1951.

Contents

Across the Bridge

The story I want to tell you has no particular point to it, maybe it isn't really a story at all, but I must tell you about it. Ten years ago there was a kind of prelude, and a few days ago the circle was completed...

A few days ago I was in a train crossing the bridge that once, before the war, had been strong and wide, as strong as the iron of Bismarck's chest on all those monuments, as inflexible as the rules of bureaucracy; a wide, four-track railway bridge over the Rhine, supported by a row of massive piers, and ten years ago I used to take the same train across that bridge three times a week: Mondays, Wednesdays, and Saturdays. In those prewar days I was an employee of the Reich Gun Dog and Retriever Association; a modest position, I was a kind of errand-boy, really. I knew nothing about dogs, of course, I haven't had much education. Three times a week I would take the train from Königstadt, where our head office was, to Gründerheim, where we had a branch office. There I would pick up urgent correspondence, money, and 'Pending Cases'. The latter were in a large manila folder. Being only a messenger, of course, I never was told what was in the folder...

In the morning I would go straight from the house to the station and catch the eight o'clock train to Gründerheim. The journey took three-quarters of an hour. Even in those days, crossing the bridge scared me. All the technical assurances of well-informed people concerning the ample load-capacity of the bridge were to no avail: I was just plain scared. The mere connection of train and bridge scared me; I am honest enough to admit it. The Rhine is very broad where we live. With a

9

quaking heart I was invariably conscious of the slight swaying of the bridge, of the ominous rocking that continued for six hundred yards. At last came the reassuring, more muffled rattle as we regained the railway embankment, and then came the vegetable plots, rows and rows of vegetable plots – and finally, just before Kahlenkatten, a house: it was to this house that I clung, so to speak, with my eyes. This house stood on solid ground; my eyes would clutch at this house.

The exterior of the house was of reddish-brown stucco, it was very clean, the window frames and ledges all picked out in dark brown. Two floors, three windows upstairs and two down, in the middle the front door with three steps leading up to it. And invariably, if it was not raining too hard, a child would be sitting on these steps, a spindly little girl of about nine or ten holding a large, clean doll and frowning up at the train. Invariably my eyes would stumble over this child, to be brought up short by the window on the left, for each time I saw a woman in there, a bucket beside her, bent double, a scrubbing cloth in her hands, laboriously washing the floor. Invariably, even when it was raining cats and dogs, even when the child was not sitting there on the steps. The woman was always there: the thin nape of her neck, betraying her as the mother of the little girl, and that movement to and fro, that typical scrubbing movement. Many a time I meant to notice the furniture, or the curtains, but my eyes were glued to this thin, eternally scrubbing woman, and before I could think about anything else the train had passed. Mondays, Wednesdays, and Saturdays, it must always have been about ten minutes past eight, for in those days the trains were nothing if not punctual. By the time the train had passed, I was left with a view of the clean rear of the house, silent and uncommunicative.

Needless to say, I began wondering about this woman and this house. All the other places we passed held little interest for me. Kahlenkatten – Bröderkotten – Suhlenheim – Gründerheim – there was nothing very interesting about these stations. My thoughts were always preoccupied with that house. Why does the woman wash and scrub three times a week, I wondered. The house didn't look at all as if there were dirty people living in it, or as if a great many visitors came and went. In fact it looked almost inhospitable, although it was clean. It was a clean and yet unwelcoming house.

But when I caught the eleven o'clock train from Gründerheim for the return trip and saw the rear of the house shortly before noon just beyond Kahlenkatten, the woman would then be washing the panes of the end window on the right. Oddly enough, on Mondays and Saturdays she would be washing the end window on the right, and on Wednesdays the middle window. Chamois in hand, she rubbed and rubbed. Round her head she wore a scarf of a dull, reddish colour. But on the way back I never saw the little girl, and now, approaching midday – it must have been a few minutes to twelve, for in those days the trains were nothing if not punctual – it was the front of the house that was silent and uncommunicative.

Although in telling my story I shall make every effort to describe only what I actually saw, presumably no one will object to the modest observation that, after three months, I permitted myself the mathematical combination that on Tuesdays, Thursdays, and Fridays the woman probably washed the other windows. This combination, modest though it was, gradually became an obsession. Sometimes, all the way from just before Kahlenkatten to Gründerheim, I would puzzle over which afternoons and mornings the other windows of the two floors were likely to get washed. In fact, I finally sat down with pencil and paper and devised a kind of cleaning timetable for myself. From what I had observed on the three mornings, I tried to figure out what was likely to get cleaned the other three afternoons and the remaining whole days. For I had the curiously fixed notion that the woman never did anything but wash and scrub. After all, I never saw her any other way, always bent double, so that I thought I could hear her laboured breathing – at ten minutes past eight; and busily rubbing with the chamois, so that I thought I could see the tip of her tongue between her tightly drawn lips – shortly before twelve.

The story of this house preyed on my mind. I started day-dreaming. This made me careless in my work. Yes, I became careless. I let my thoughts wander too often. One day I even forgot the 'Pending Cases' folder. I drew down upon my head the wrath of the District Manager of the Reich Gun Dog and Retriever Association. He sent for me; he was quivering with indignation. 'Grabowski,' he said to me, 'I hear you forgot the "Pending Cases". Orders are orders, Grabowski.' When I maintained a stubborn silence, the boss became more severe. 'Messenger Grabowski, I'm warning you. The Reich Gun Dog and Retriever Association has no use for forgetful employees, you know. We can look elsewhere for qualified staff.' He looked at me menacingly, but then he suddenly became human. 'Have you something on your mind?' I admitted in a low voice: 'Yes.' 'What is it?' he asked kindly. I merely shook my head. 'Can I help? Tell me what I can do.'

'Give me a day off, sir,' I asked diffidently, 'that's all I ask.' He nodded magnanimously. 'Done! And don't take what I said too seriously. Anybody can make one mistake, we've always been quite satisfied with you . . .'

My heart leaped with joy. This interview took place on a Wednesday. And the following day, Thursday, was to be my day off. I had it all figured out. I caught the eight o'clock train, trembling more with impatience than with fear as we crossed the bridge: there she was, washing the front steps. I caught the next train back from Kahlenkatten and passed her house just about nine: top floor, middle window, front. I rode back and forth four times that day and had the whole Thursday timetable complete: front steps, middle window top floor front, middle window top floor back, attic, front room top. As I passed the house for the last time at six o'clock, I saw a little man's stooped figure digging humbly away in the garden. The child, holding the clean doll, was watching him like a jaileress. The woman was not in sight . . .

But all this happened ten years ago, before the war. A few days ago I crossed that bridge again by train. My God, how far away

my thoughts had been when I got onto the train at Königstadt!
I had forgotten the whole business. Our train was made up of
boxcars, and as we approached the Rhine a strange thing
happened: one after another the boxcars ahead of us fell silent.
It was quite extraordinary, as if the whole train of fifteen or
twenty cars were a series of lights going out one after another.
And we could hear a horrible, hollow rattle, a kind of windy
rattle; and suddenly it sounded as if little hammers were being
tapped against the floor of our boxcar, and we fell silent too,
and there it was: nothing, nothing . . . nothing; left and right
there was nothing, a ghastly void . . . in the distance the grassy
banks of the Rhine . . . boats . . . water, but one didn't dare look
too far out: just looking made one giddy. Nothing, nothing
whatever! I could tell from the white face of a silent farmer's
wife that she was praying, other people were lighting cigarettes
with trembling hands; even the men playing cards in the corner
had fallen silent . . .

Then we could hear the cars up front riding over solid ground
again, and we all had the same thought: they've made it. If
something happens to the train, maybe those people can jump
out, but we were in the last car but one, and it was almost a
foregone conclusion that we would plunge into the river. The
conviction was there in our eyes and in our pale faces. The
temporary bridge was no wider than the tracks, in fact the tracks
themselves were the bridge, and the side of the boxcar hung
out over the bridge into space, and the bridge rocked as if it
were about to tip us off into space . . .

But then all of a sudden there was a firmer rattle, we could
hear it coming closer, quite distinctly, and then under our car
too it became somehow deeper, more substantial, this rattle, we
breathed again and dared to look out: there were vegetable plots!
Oh, may God bless vegetable plots! And suddenly I realized
where we were, and my heart throbbed queerly the closer we
came to Kahlenkatten. For me there was but one question:
would that house still be standing? And then I saw it, first from
a distance through the delicate sparse green of a few trees in the

vegetable plots, the red façade of the house, still very clean, coming closer and closer. I was gripped by an indefinable emotion. Everything, the past of ten years ago and everything that had happened since then, raged within me in a frenzied, uncontrollable turmoil. And then the house came right up close, with giant strides, and then I saw her, the woman: she was washing the front steps. No, it wasn't her, those legs were younger, a little heavier, but she had the same movements, those jerky, thrusting movements as she pushed the scrubbing cloth to and fro. My heart stood still, my heart marked time. Then the woman turned her face for just a moment, and instantly I recognized the little girl of ten years ago; that pinched, spidery, frowning face, and in the expression on her face something rather sour, something disagreeably sour like stale salad . . .

As my heart slowly started beating again, it struck me that today was in fact Thursday . . .

My Pal with the Long Hair

It was a funny thing: exactly five minutes before the raid started I had a feeling something was wrong . . . I looked warily round, then 'strolled along the Rhine towards the station, and it didn't surprise me at all to see the jeeps come dashing up full of red-capped military police who proceeded to surround the block, cordon it off, and begin their search. It all happened incredibly fast. I stood just outside the cordon and calmly lighted a cigarette. Everything was done so quietly. Quantities of cigarettes landed on the ground. Too bad, I thought . . . instinctively making a rough calculation as to the cash that must be lying around there. The truck rapidly filled up with the ones they had nabbed. Franz was among them . . . he gestured to me from a distance in a resigned kind of way, as much as to say: Just my luck. One of the policemen turned round to look at me, so I left. But slowly, very slowly. Hell, let them pick me up too, I couldn't care less.

I was in no mood to go back to my room so I continued my stroll towards the station. I flicked a pebble aside with my stick. The sun was warm, and a cool, soft breeze blew from the Rhine.

At the station buffet I gave Fritz, the waiter, the two hundred cigarettes and stuffed the money into my hip pocket. I had no more to sell now, just a packet for myself. In spite of the crowds jamming the place, I managed to find a seat and ordered a bowl of soup and some bread. Again I saw Fritz signalling me from across the room, but I didn't feel like getting up, so he came hurrying across to me, with little Mausbach, the contact man, in tow. They both seemed pretty excited. 'Man, are you ever a cool customer!' muttered Fritz and, shaking his head, he went off, leaving the field to little Mausbach.

Mausbach was all out of breath. 'For God's sake, man,' he stammered, 'beat it! They've searched your room and found the dope . . . Oh my God!' H was almost choking. I patted him reassuringly on the shoulder and gave him twenty marks. 'That's O.K.,' I said, and off he trotted. But I suddenly had an idea and called him back. 'Listen, Heini,' I said, 'd'you suppose you could find a safe place for my books and overcoat? They're in my room. I'll come by again in a couple of weeks, O.K.? You can keep the rest of my things.' He nodded. I could trust him. I knew that.

Too bad, I thought again . . . eight thousand marks down the drain. Nowhere, nowhere could a fellow feel safe.

A few inquisitive glances came my way as I slowly sat down again and nonchalantly reached for my pocket. Then the buzzing of the crowds closed over me, and I knew that nowhere else could I have been as marvellously alone with my thoughts as here, surrounded by all these swarms of people milling around in the station buffet.

All at once I was aware that my gaze, as it more or less automatically circled the room without taking anything in, invariably halted at the same spot, as if attracted to it by some magnetic spell. Each time, as my gaze casually toured the room, there was that spot where my eye was caught for a second before sliding hastily over it. I awoke as if from a deep sleep and, now with seeing eyes, looked in that direction.

Two tables away from me sat a girl wearing a light-coloured coat, a tan beret on her dark hair, reading a newspaper. I could see very little of her: her shoulders hunching slightly forward, a tiny portion of her nose, and her slender, motionless hands. And I could see her legs too, beautiful legs, slim and . . . yes, clean. I don't know how long I stared at her; from time to time I caught sight of the narrow oval of her face as she turned a page. Suddenly she raised her head and for a moment looked me straight in the face with her large grey eyes, grave and detached, then resumed her reading.

That brief glance found its mark.

Patiently, yet conscious of my beating heart, I kept my eyes fixed on her until she finally finished the paper, leaned her arms on the table and, with a strangely despairing gesture, took a sip from her glass of beer.

Now I could see her whole face. A pale face, very pale, a small fine-drawn mouth, and a straight, patrician nose ... but her eyes, those huge, grave, grey eyes! Like a mourning veil her black hair hung down in dark waves to her shoulders.

I don't know how long I stared at her, whether it was twenty minutes, an hour, or longer. Each time she ran her eyes over my face, her glance became more uneasy, more brief, but her face showed none of the indignation girls usually show on such occasions. Uneasiness, yes ... and fear.

God knows I didn't want to make her uneasy or afraid, but I couldn't take my eyes off her.

At last she got up abruptly, slung a worn haversack over her shoulder, and quickly left the buffet. I followed her. Without turning round she went up the steps towards the barrier. I kept her firmly, firmly within my line of vision as, with barely a pause, I hurriedly bought a platform ticket. She had a good head start on me, and I had to tuck my stick under my arm and try to run a little. I very nearly lost her in the dimly lit underpass leading up to the platform. I found her up at the top leaning against the remains of a bombed-out platform shelter. She was staring fixedly at the tracks. Not *once* did she turn around.

A chill wind from the Rhine was blowing right into the station. Evening came. A lot of people with packs and rucksacks, boxes and suitcases, stood about on the platform with harassed expressions. They turned their heads in dismay to where the wind was blowing from, and shivered. Ahead of them, dark blue and tranquil, yawned the great semicircle of the sky, punctured by the iron latticework of the station roof.

I limped slowly up and down, now and then glancing towards the girl to make sure she hadn't disappeared. But she was still there, still leaning straight-legged against the ruined wall, her eyes fixed on the flat, black trough in which the shining rails were embedded.

17

My Pal with the Long Hair

At last the train backed slowly into the station. While I was looking towards the engine, the girl had jumped onto the moving train and disappeared into a compartment. I lost sight of her for several minutes among all the knots of people jostling their way into the compartments, but before long I glimpsed the tan beret in the last car. I got in and sat down right opposite her, so close that our knees were almost touching. When she looked at me, very gravely and quietly, her brows slightly puckered, the expression in her great grey eyes told me that she knew I had been following her the whole time. Again and again my eyes fastened helplessly on her face as the train sped into the oncoming evening. My lips refused to utter a word. The fields sank from view, and the villages gradually became shrouded in the night. I felt cold. Where was I going to sleep tonight, I thought . . . where would I ever be able to breathe easily again? Ah, if I could only bury my face in that black hair. That was all I asked, I asked for nothing more . . . I lit a cigarette. She cast a fleeting but oddly alert glance at the package. I merely held it out to her, saying huskily: 'Help yourself,' and felt as if my heart were going to jump out of my throat. She hesitated for a fraction of a second, and in spite of the darkness I saw her momentarily blush. Then she took one. She pulled deeply and hungrily on the cigarette as she smoked.

'You are very generous.' Her voice was dark-toned and brusque. A few minutes later I heard the conductor in the next compartment, and as if at a signal we instantly threw ourselves back into our corners and pretended to be asleep. But I could see through my half-open lids that she was laughing. I watched the conductor as he shone his glaring flashlight onto the tickets and checked them. And the next moment the light was shining right into my face. I could feel from the way the light wavered that he was hesitating. Then the light fell on her. How pale she was, and how sad the white surface of her forehead.

A stout woman sitting beside me pulled at the conductor's sleeve and whispered something in his ear. I caught the words: 'American cigarettes . . . black market . . . no ticket . . .,' to which the conductor responded by giving me a spiteful jab in the ribs.

There was silence in the compartment as I asked her quietly where she was going. She named a town. I bought two tickets for the place and paid the fine. The silence of the other passengers, after the conductor had gone, was icy and scornful. But her voice was strange, warm and yet mocking, as she asked:

'So you're going there too?'

'Oh, I might as well get off there. I have friends there. I've got no permanent home ...'

'I see,' was all she said. She leaned back in her corner, and in the close darkness I could only glimpse her face whenever a light outside rushed by.

It was pitch-dark by the time we got out. Dark and warm. And when we emerged from the station the small town was already fast asleep. The little houses slept safe and sound beneath the gentle trees. 'I'll go with you,' I said hoarsely, 'it's so dark you can't see a thing ...'

But suddenly she stopped. It was under a street lamp. She fixed me with a long, wide-eyed stare and said in a strained voice: 'If only I knew where I was going.' Her face moved slightly, like a scarf stirred by a breeze. No, we did not kiss ... We walked slowly out through the town and eventually crawled into a haystack. I had no friends here, of course: I was as much a stranger in this silent town as in any other. When it got chilly towards morning, I crept close beside her, and she covered me with part of her thin, skimpy coat. And so we warmed each other with our breath and our blood.

We have been together ever since – in these hard times.

The Man with the Knives

Jupp held the knife by the tip of the blade, letting it joggle idly up and down; it was a long, tapering bread knife, obviously razor-sharp. With a sudden flick of the wrist he tossed the knife into the air: up it went, whirring like a propeller; the shining blade glittered like a golden fish in a sheaf of lingering sunbeams, struck the ceiling, lost its spin, and plunged down straight at Jupp's head. In a flash Jupp had placed a wooden block on his head; the knife scored into the wood and remained embedded there, gently swaying. Jupp removed the block from his head, withdrew the knife, and flung it with a gesture of annoyance at the door, where it stuck, quivering, in the frame until it gradually stopped vibrating and fell to the floor . . .

'It makes me sick,' said Jupp quietly. 'I've been working on the logical assumption that people who've paid for their tickets really want to see a show where life and limb are at stake – like at the Roman circuses – they want to be convinced of at least the *possibility* of bloodshed, know what I mean?'

He picked up the knife and tossed it neatly against the top crossbar of the window, with such force that the panes rattled and threatened to fall out of the crumbling putty. This throw – confident and unerring – took me back to those hours of semi-darkness in the past when he had thrown his pocket-knife against the dugout post, from bottom to top and down again.

'I'll do anything,' he went on, 'to give the customers a thrill. I'll even cut off my ears, only it's hard to find anyone to stick them back on again. Here, I want to show you something.'

He opened the door for me, and we went out into the hallway. A few shreds of wallpaper still clung to the walls where the glue was too stubborn for them to be ripped off and used for lighting the stove. After passing through a mouldering bathroom we emerged onto a kind of terrace, its concrete floor cracked and moss-covered.

Jupp pointed upward.

'The higher the knife goes, of course, the greater the effect. But I need some resistance up there for the thing to strike against and lose momentum so that it can come hurtling down straight at my useless skull. Look!' He pointed up to where the iron girders of a ruined balcony stuck out into the air.

'This is where I used to practise. For a whole year. Watch!' He sent the knife soaring upward: it rose with marvellous symmetry and evenness, seeming to climb as smoothly and effortlessly as a bird: then it struck one of the girders, shot down with breathtaking speed, and crashed into the wooden block. The impact itself must have been terrific. Jupp didn't bat an eyelid. The knife had buried itself a couple of inches in the wood.

'But that's fantastic!' I cried. 'It's absolutely sensational, they'll have to like it – what an act!'

Jupp nonchalantly withdrew the knife from the wood, grasped it by the handle and made a thrust in the air.

'Oh they like it all right, they pay me twelve marks a night, and between the main acts they let me play around a bit with the knife. But the act's not elaborate enough. A man, a knife, a block of wood, don't you see? I ought to have a half-naked girl so I can send the knife spinning a hair's breadth past her nose. That'd make the crowd go wild. But try and find that kind of a girl!'

He went ahead as we returned to his room. He placed the knife carefully on the table, the wooden block beside it, and rubbed his hands. We sat down on the crate beside the stove and were silent. Taking some bread out of my pocket, I said: 'Be my guest.'

'Thanks, I will, but let me make some coffee. Then you can come along and watch my performance.'

He put some more wood in the stove and set the pot over the opening. 'It's infuriating,' he said. 'Maybe I look too serious, a bit like a sergeant still, eh?'

'Nonsense, you never were a sergeant. D'you smile when they clap?'

'Of course – and bow too.'

'I couldn't. I couldn't smile in a cemetery.'

'That's a great mistake: a cemetery's the very place *to* smile.'

'I don't get it.'

'Because they aren't dead. They're none of them dead, see?'

'I see, all right, but I don't believe it.'

'There's still a bit of the lieutenant about you after all. Well, in that case it just takes longer, of course. The point is, I'm only too glad if they enjoy it. They're burned out inside, I give them a bit of a thrill and get paid for it. Perhaps one of them, just one, will go home and not forget me. "That man with the knife, for Christ's sake, he wasn't scared, and I'm scared all the time, for Christ's sake," maybe that's what he'll say because they're all scared, all the time. They trail their fear behind them like a heavy shadow, and it makes me happy if they can forget about it and laugh a little. Isn't that reason enough to smile?'

I said nothing, my eyes on the water, waiting for it to boil. Jupp poured the boiling water onto the coffee in the brown enamel pot, and we took turns drinking from the brown enamel pot and shared my bread. Outside the mild dusk began to fall, flowing into the room like soft grey milk.

'What are *you* doing these days, by the way?' asked Jupp.

'Nothing . . . just getting by.'

'A hard way to make a living.'

'Right – for this loaf of bread I had to collect a hundred bricks and clean them. Casual labour.'

'Hm . . . Want to see another of my tricks?'

In response to my nod he stood up, switched on the light, and went over to the wall, where he pushed aside a kind of rug, disclosing the rough outline of a man drawn in charcoal on the reddish colour-wash: a strange lump protruded from what was supposed to be the head, probably signifying a hat. On closer inspection I saw that the man had been drawn on a skilfully camouflaged door. I watched expectantly as Jupp proceeded to pull out a handsome little brown leather suitcase from under the miserable affair that served as his bed and put it on the table. Before opening it he came over and placed four cigarette butts in front of me. 'Roll those into two thin ones,' he said.

I moved my seat so that I could watch him as well as get a bit more of the gentle warmth from the stove. While I was carefully pulling the butts apart on the bread paper spread over my knees, Jupp had snapped open the lock of the suitcase and pulled out an odd-looking object: one of those flannel bags consisting of a series of pockets in which our mothers used to keep their table silver. He deftly untied the ribbon and let the bundle unroll across the table to reveal a dozen wood-handled knives, the kind that, in the days when our mothers danced the waltz, were known as 'hunting cutlery'.

I divided the tobacco shreds scrupulously in half onto the two cigarette papers and rolled them. 'Here,' I said.

'Here,' Jupp said too, and: 'Thanks,' bringing over the flannel bag for me to look at.

'This is all I managed to salvage from my parents' belongings. Almost everything was burned or lost in the rubble, and the rest stolen. When I got back from P.O.W. camp I was really on my beam ends, didn't own a thing in the world – until one day a dignified old lady, a friend of my mother's, tracked me down and brought along this nice suitcase. A few days before my mother was killed in an air raid she had left it with the old lady to be looked after, and it had survived. Funny, isn't it? But of course we know that when people panic they try to save the strangest things. Never the essential ones. So then at least I was the owner of the contents of this suitcase: the brown enamel pot, twelve forks, twelve knives, and twelve spoons, and the long bread knife. I sold the spoons and forks, living off the proceeds for a year, and practised with the knives, thirteen of them. Watch . . .'

I passed him the spill I had used to light my cigarette. Jupp stuck his cigarette to his lower lip, fastened the ribbon of the flannel bag to a button on the shoulder of his jacket, and let the flannel unroll along his arm like some exotic panoply of war. Then with incredible speed he whisked the knives out of their pockets, and before I could follow his movements he had thrown all twelve like lightning against the dim human outline, which reminded me of those sinister, shambling figures that came lurching at us towards the end of the war from every billboard, every corner, harbingers of defeat and destruction. Two knives were sticking out of the man's hat, two over each shoulder, and the others, three a side, along the dangling arms . . .

'Fantastic!' I cried. 'Fantastic! But you've got your act right there, with a bit of dramatizing.'

'All I need is a man, better still a girl. But I know I'll never find anyone,' he said with a sigh, plucking the knives out of the door and slipping them carefully back into their pockets. 'The girls are too scared and the men want too much money. Can't blame them, of course, it's a risky business.'

Once again he flung the knives back at the door in such a way as to split the entire black figure accurately down the middle with dazzling symmetry. The thirteenth knife, the big one, stuck like a deadly arrow just where the man's heart should have been.

Jupp took a final puff of the thin, tobacco-filled roll of paper and threw the scant remains behind the stove.

'Let's go,' he said, 'it's time we were off.' He stuck his head out of the window, muttered something about 'damned rain', and added: 'It's a few minutes to eight, I'm on at eight-thirty.'

While he was packing the knives away in the suitcase I stood with my face by the open window. Decaying villas seemed to be whimpering softly in the rain, and from behind a wall of swaying poplars came the screech of the streetcar. But nowhere could I see a clock.

'How d'you know what time it is?'

'Instinct – that's part of my training.'

I gaped at him. First he helped me on with my coat and then put on his windbreaker. My shoulder is slightly paralyzed and I can't move my arms beyond a certain radius, just far enough to clean bricks. We put on our caps and went out into the dingy corridor, and I was glad to hear at least some voices in the house, laughter, and a subdued murmuring.

'It's like this,' said Jupp as we went down the stairs. 'What I've tried to do is trace certain cosmic laws. Watch.' He put the suitcase down on a stair and spread his arms, an Icarus poised for flight in the way the ancient Greeks used to show him. His matter-of-fact expression assumed a strangely cool and dreamlike quality, something between obsession and detachment, something magical, that I found quite spine-chilling. 'Like this,' he said softly, 'I simply reach out into the atmosphere, I feel my hands getting longer and longer, reaching out into a dimension governed by different laws, they push through a ceiling, and beyond are strange, spell-binding tensions – I just take hold of them, that's all . . . and then I seize their laws, snatch them away, part-thief, part-lover, and carry them off.' He clenched his fists, drawing them close to his body. 'Let's go,' he said, and his expression was its usual matter-of-fact self. I followed him in a daze . . .

Outside a chill rain was falling softly and steadily. We turned up our collars and withdrew shivering into ourselves. The mist of twilight was surging through the streets, already tinged with the bluish darkness of night. In several basements among the bombed-out villas a meagre light was burning under the towering black weight of a great ruin. The street gradually became a muddy path where to left and right, in the opaque twilight, shacks loomed up in the scrawny gardens like junks afloat in a shallow backwater. We crossed the streetcar tracks, plunged into the maze of narrow streets on the city's outskirts, where among piles of rubble and garbage a few houses still stand intact in the dirt, until we emerged suddenly into a busy street. The tide of the crowds carried us along for a bit, until we turned a corner into a dark side street where a garish illuminated sign saying 'The Seven Mills' was reflected in the glistening asphalt.

The foyer of the vaudeville theatre was empty. The performance had already begun, and the buzzing of the audience penetrated the shabby red drapes.

With a laugh Jupp pointed to a photograph in a display case, where he was shown in cowboy costume between two coyly smiling dancers whose breasts were hung with sparkling tinsel. Beneath was the caption: 'The Man with the Knives.'

'Come on,' said Jupp, and before I grasped what was happening I found myself being dragged through a half-hidden door. We climbed a poorly lit staircase, narrow and winding, the smell of sweat and greasepaint indicating the nearness of the stage. Jupp was ahead – suddenly he halted in a turn of the stairs, put down the suitcase, and, gripping me by the shoulders, asked in a hushed voice:

'Are you game?'

I had been expecting this question for so long that when it came its suddenness startled me. I must have looked non-plussed, for after a pause he said: 'Well?'

I still hesitated, and suddenly we heard a great roar of laughter that seemed to come pouring out of the narrow passage and engulf us like a tidal wave; it was so overwhelming that I jumped and involuntarily shuddered.

'I'm scared,' I whispered.

'So am I. Don't you trust me'

'Sure I do ... but ... let's go,' I said hoarsely, pushing past him and adding, with the courage born of despair: 'I've nothing to lose.'

We emerged onto a narrow corridor with a number of rough plywood cubicles right and left. A few oddly garbed figures were scurrying about, and through an opening in the flimsy wings I could see a clown on the stage, his enormous mouth wide open; once again the roar of the crowd's laughter engulfed us, but Jupp pulled me through a door and shut it behind us. I looked around. The cubicle was tiny, practically bare. On the wall was a mirror, Jupp's cowboy costume hung on the single nail, and on a rickety chair lay an old deck of cards. Jupp moved with nervous haste; he took my wet coat from me, flung the cowboy suit onto the chair, hung up my coat, then his windbreaker. Over the top of the partition I could see an electric clock on a fake red Doric column, showing twenty-five after eight.

'Five minutes,' muttered Jupp, slipping into his costume. 'Shall we rehearse it?'

Just then someone knocked on the cubicle door and called: 'You're on!'

Jupp buttoned up his shirt and stuck a ten-gallon hat on his head. With a forced laugh I cried: 'D'you expect a condemned man to rehearse his own hanging?'

Jupp snatched up the suitcase and dragged me through the door. Outside stood a bald-headed man watching the clown going through his final motions on the stage. Jupp whispered something to the man that I didn't catch, the man glanced up with a start, looked at me, looked at Jupp, and shook his head vehemently. And again Jupp whispered something to him.

I couldn't have cared less. Let them impale me alive. I had a crippled shoulder, I had just finished a thin cigarette, tomorrow I would get three-quarters of a loaf for seventy-five bricks. But tomorrow . . . The applause almost blew down the wings. The clown, his face tired and contorted, staggered towards us through the opening of the wings, stood there for a few seconds looking morose, and then went back onto the stage, where he smiled graciously and bowed. The orchestra played a fanfare. Jupp was still whispering to the bald-headed man. Three times the clown came back into the wings and three times he went out on to the stage and bowed, smiling.

Then the orchestra struck up a march and, suitcase in hand, Jupp strode smartly out onto the stage. His appearance was greeted with subdued clapping. Weary-eyed I watched Jupp fasten the playing cards onto nails that were already in place and then impale each card with a knife, one by one, precisely in the centre. The applause became more animated, but not enthusiastic. Then, to a muffled roll of drums, he performed his trick with the bread knife and the block of wood, and underneath all my indifference I was aware that the act really was a bit thin. Across from me, on the other side of the stage, a few scantily dressed girls stood watching . . . And suddenly the bald-headed man seized me by the shoulder, dragged me onto the stage, greeted

Jupp with a grandiose sweep of the arm and, in the spurious voice of a policeman, said: 'Good evening, Mr Borgalevsky.'

'Good evening, Mr Erdmenger,' replied Jupp, likewise in ceremonious tones.

'I've brought you a horse-thief, a proper scoundrel, Mr Borgalevsky, for you to tickle a bit with your shiny knives before we hang him . . . a real scoundrel . . .' I found his voice totally ridiculous, pathetically artificial, like paper flowers or the cheapest kind of greasepaint. I glanced at the audience, and from that moment on, faced by that glimmering, slavering, hydra-headed monster crouching there in the dark ready to spring, I simply switched off.

I didn't give a damn, I was dazzled by the glare of the spotlight, and in my threadbare suit and shabby shoes I probably made a pretty convincing horse-thief.

'Oh, leave him here with me, Mr Erdmenger, I know how to deal with him.'

'Splendid, let him have it, and don't spare the knives.'

Jupp took hold of me by the collar while the grinning Erdmenger swaggered off the stage. Someone threw a rope onto the stage, and Jupp proceeded to tie me by the feet to a cardboard column that had a fake door, painted blue, propped up behind it. I was aware of something like an ecstasy of insensibility. To my right I heard the eerie stirring of the tense audience, and I realized Jupp had been right in speaking of its bloodlust. Its thirst quivered on the sickly, stale air, and the orchestra, with its facile drum-roll, its muffled lasciviousness, heightened the effect of grisly tragicomedy in which real blood would flow, stage-blood that had been paid for . . . I stared straight ahead, letting my body sag, the rope being so firmly tied that it held me upright. The drum-roll became softer and softer as Jupp calmly pulled his knives out of the playing cards and slipped them back into their pockets, from time to time casting melodramatic glances my way as if to size me up. Then, having packed away all his knives, he turned to the audience and in the same odiously stagey voice announced: 'Ladies and gentlemen, I am now about to outline this young man with knives, but I wish to demonstrate to you that I do not throw blunt knives . . .' He produced a piece of string, and with perfect sangfroid removed one knife after another from its pocket, touched the string with each, cutting it into twelve pieces, and then replaced the knives one by one in their pockets.

While all this was going on I looked far beyond him, far beyond the wings, far beyond the half-naked girls, into another life, it seemed . . .

The tension in the audience was electrifying. Jupp came over to me, pretended to adjust the rope, and said softly into my ear: 'Don't move a muscle, and trust me . . .'

This added delay nearly broke the tension, it was threatening to peter out, but he suddenly stretched out his arms, letting his hands flutter like hovering birds, and his face assumed that look of magical concentration that I had marvelled at on the stairs. He appeared to be casting a spell over the audience too with this sorcerer's pose. I seemed to hear a strange, unearthly groan and realized that this was a warning signal for me.

Withdrawing my gaze from limitless horizons, I looked at Jupp, now standing opposite me so that our eyes were on a level; he raised his hand, moving it slowly towards a pocket, and again I realized that this was a signal for me. I stood completely still and closed my eyes . . .

It was a glorious feeling, lasting maybe two seconds, I'm not sure. Listening to the swish of the knives and the short sharp hiss of air as they plunged into the fake blue door, I felt as if I were walking along a very narrow plank over a bottomless abyss. I walked with perfect confidence, yet felt all the thrill of danger . . . I was afraid, yet absolutely certain that I would not fall; I was not counting, yet I opened my eyes at the very moment when the last knife pierced the door beside my right hand . . .

A storm of applause jerked me bolt upright. I opened my eyes properly to find myself looking into Jupp's white face: he had rushed over to me and was untying the rope with trembling hands. Then he pulled me into the centre of the stage, right up to the very edge. He bowed, and I bowed; as the applause swelled he pointed to me and I to him; then he smiled at me, I smiled at him, and we both bowed smiling to the audience.

Back in the cubicle not a word was said. Jupp threw the perforated playing cards onto the chair, took my coat off the nail and helped me on with it. Then he hung his cowboy costume back on the nail, pulled on his windbreaker, and we put on our caps. As I opened the door the little bald-headed man rushed up to us shouting: 'I'm raising you to forty marks!' He handed Jupp some cash. I realized then that Jupp was my boss, and I smiled; he looked at me too and smiled.

Jupp took my arm, and side by side we walked down the narrow, poorly lit stairs that smelled of stale greasepaint. When we reached the foyer Jupp said with a laugh: 'Now let's go and buy some cigarettes and bread . . .'

But it was not till an hour later that I realized I now had a proper profession, a profession where all I needed to do was stand still and dream a little. For twelve or twenty seconds. I was the man who has knives thrown at him . . .

Rise, My Love, Rise

Her name on the rough-hewn cross was no longer legible; the cardboard coffin lid had already collapsed, and where a few weeks ago there had been a mound there was now a hollow in which soiled, rotting flowers and faded ribbons, mixed with fir needles and bare twigs, formed a nauseating pulp. Someone must have stolen the candle ends . . .

'Rise, my love,' I whispered, 'rise,' and my tears mingled with the rain, the monotonous murmuring rain that had been falling for weeks. –

I closed my eyes: I was afraid my wish might come true. In my mind's eye I distinctly saw the sagging cardboard lid that must now be lying on her breast, caving in beneath the wet piles of cold, greedy earth that were forcing their way past it into the coffin.

I bent down to remove the bedraggled flowers and ribbons from the sticky clay, and all at once I was aware of a shadow springing out of the ground behind me, with a sudden leap, as a flame sometimes flares up out of a banked fire.

I hastily crossed myself, threw down the flowers, and hurried to the exit. The opaque dusk was welling out of the narrow, shrub-bordered paths, and as I reached the main avenue I heard the sound of the bell summoning visitors from the cemetery. But I heard no footsteps approaching, saw no figure behind me, I just sensed that impalpable yet undeniable shadow at my heels . . .

I quickened my pace, clanged the rusty gate behind me, crossed the grassy roundabout at the intersection where an overturned streetcar lay exposing its bloated belly to the rain, the accursed gentleness of the rain drumming on the great metal box . . .

The rain had soaked through my shoes, but I was aware of

neither cold nor damp, a hectic fever was driving the blood into the furthest extremities of my limbs, and through the fear that was breathing down my neck I was conscious of that strange gratification that comes from illness and grief . . .

Between rows of shacks, their chimneys emitting wisps of smoke, between ingeniously patched-up fences surrounding grey-black fields, past rotting telegraph poles that appeared to sway in the dusk, my route took me through what seemed to be infinite suburban regions of despair; stepping heedlessly into puddles, I walked faster and faster towards the city's distant, jagged silhouette looming upon the horizon, among the murky twilight clouds, like a labyrinth of misery.

Enormous black ruins sprang up left and right, strangely oppressive sounds assailed me from feebly lighted windows; more fields of black earth, more houses, ruined villas – and horror, as well as my fever, was eating its way deeper and deeper into my very bones as I experienced a nightmarish sensation: behind me it was almost dark, while ahead of me dusk was deepening in the familiar way; behind me night was falling, I was dragging the night after me, trailing it across the distant edge of the horizon, and wherever my foot touched the ground, darkness fell. Not that I saw any of this, but I knew: from the grave of my love, where I had invoked the shadow, I was dragging the relentlessly drooping sail of the night behind me.

The world seemed devoid of human life: a vast, muddy suburban plane, a low mountain range formed by the ruins of the city that had seemed so far away and was now, with unaccountable speed, suddenly so much closer. From time to time I halted, and I could sense the dark presence behind me, waiting, reining itself in, mocking me as it hesitated, and then driving me on with gentle, irresistible pressure.

And now I realized that the sweat was pouring down my whole body; it was an effort to walk, the weight I was dragging, the weight of the world, was heavy. Invisible ropes bound me to it, it to me, and now it was straining and tugging at me as a slipping load forces the exhausted mule inescapably into the abyss. I summoned all my strength to resist those invisible cords, my steps became short and unsteady, like a desperate animal I hurled myself into the strangling harness: my legs seemed to sink into the ground but I still had strength enough to keep my body upright, until I suddenly felt I could hold out no longer, that I was compelled to stop where I was, that the weight had the power to root me to the spot; and the next moment I felt I was losing my footing. I screamed and threw myself once more into the impalpable reins – I toppled forward onto my face, the bond was sundered, an unutterably exquisite freedom was behind me, and ahead was a shining expanse, and she was standing there, she who had been lying in that sordid grave under bedraggled flowers, and this time it was she who said to me, with a smile on her face: 'Rise, my love, rise . . .' but I had already risen and was walking towards her . . .

That Time We Were in Odessa

That time we were in Odessa it was very cold. Every morning we drove in great rattling trucks along cobbled streets to the airfield, where we waited, shivering, for the great grey birds that came lumbering across the tarmac; but the first two days, just as we were boarding, an order came through cancelling the flight due to bad weather – the fog over the Black Sea was too thick or the clouds were too low – and we climbed onto the great rattling trucks again and drove along cobbled streets back to barracks.

The barracks were huge, dirty, and louse-ridden; we sat about on the floor or sprawled over the stained tables playing cards, or sang and waited for a chance to sneak into town. There were a lot of soldiers waiting there, and the city was off limits. The first two days we tried to slip out, but they caught us, and we were given K.P. duty and had to carry the heavy scalding coffee urns and unload the bread, while a paymaster, wearing a magnificent fur coat intended for the front lines, stood by counting to see that no one pinched a loaf, and to us it looked as though the paymaster was concerned less with paying than with counting. The sky was still cloudy and dark over Odessa, and the sentries sauntered up and down in front of the black, grimy barrack walls.

The third day we waited till it was quite dark and then simply walked to the gates: when the sentry stopped us we said 'Seltchini Commando,' and he let us through. There were three of us, Kurt, Erich, and myself, and we walked along very slowly. It was only four o'clock and already quite dark. All we had really wanted was to get outside those great, black, grimy walls, and now that we were outside we would almost rather have been inside again. We hadn't been in the army more than eight weeks and were very scared, but we also knew that if we had been inside again we would most certainly have wanted to get out, and then it would have been impossible, and it was only four o'clock, and we couldn't sleep because of the lice and the singing, and also because we dreaded and at the same time hoped that the next morning might bring good flying weather, and they would fly us out to the Crimea, where we were supposed to die. We didn't want to die, and we didn't want to go to the Crimea, but neither did we want to spend the whole day cooped up in those grimy, black barracks that smelled of ersatz coffee and where they were forever unloading bread for the front and where paymasters in coats intended for the front lines stood around and counted to see that no one pinched a loaf.

I don't know what we wanted. We walked very slowly along that dark, uneven road on the outskirts of the city. Between unlighted, low houses, the night was contained by a few rotting fence posts, and somewhere beyond lay what seemed to be waste land, waste land just like at home, where people believe a road is going to be built, where they dig sewers and fiddle around with surveying instruments, and nothing ever comes of it, and they toss out rubbish, cinders, and garbage, and grass grows again, coarse, wild grass, and rank weeds, and the sign saying 'No Dumping' is hidden by all the rubbish they have dumped around it . . .

We walked along very slowly because it was still so early. In the darkness we met soldiers heading for the barracks, and there were others coming from the barracks who overtook us. We were scared of the patrols and would have liked to turn back, but we knew that once we were back in barracks we would really be desperate, and it was better to be scared than merely desperate inside those black, grimy barrack walls, where they were forever carrying coffee around and unloading bread for the front, forever unloading bread for the front, and where the paymasters got themselves up in fur coats while we shivered with cold.

Now and again a house to the left or right showed a dim yellow light, and we could hear shrill voices, high-pitched, foreign, scary. And suddenly in the darkness there was a brightly lit window, a lot of noise came from inside, and we heard soldiers' voices singing: 'Ah, the sunshine of Mexico!'

We pushed open the door and went in: the air was warm and blue with smoke, and there were soldiers, eight or ten of them, some with women, and they were all drinking and singing, and one of the soldiers burst out laughing as we entered. We were young, and short, the shortest in the whole company; our uniforms were brand-new, the synthetic fibres pricked our arms and legs and the long underwear made our bare skin itch terribly, and the sweaters were brand-new and prickly too.

Kurt, the shortest, went ahead and picked a table; he was an apprentice in a leather factory, and he had told us where the hides came from, although that was a trade secret, and he had even told us the profit they made, although that was a really strict trade secret. We sat down beside him.

A very dark, fat woman, with a good-natured face, came out from behind the bar and asked us what we wanted to drink; since we had heard that everything was very expensive in Odessa we first asked how much the wine was.

'Five marks a carafe,' she replied, and we ordered three carafes. We had lost a lot of money at cards and had divided up what we had left: each of us had ten marks. Some of the soldiers were eating too, roast meat, still steaming, on slices of white bread, and sausages smelling of garlic; we suddenly realized we were hungry, and when the woman brought the wine we asked the price of the food. She told us the sausages were five marks and meat on bread eight; it was fresh pork, she said, but we ordered three sausages. Some of the soldiers were kissing the women or quite openly hugging them, and we didn't know where to look.

The sausages were hot and greasy, and the wine was very sour. When we had finished the sausages we didn't know what to do next. We had nothing more to say to each other; for two weeks we had lain side by side in the troop train and exchanged

36

confidences. Kurt had been in a leather factory, Erich was from a farm, and I had come straight from school. We were still scared, but we weren't cold any more . . .

The soldiers who had been kissing the women now buckled on their belts and went out with the women – three girls with round, friendly faces, giggling and twittering, but they went off now with six soldiers, I think it was six, five anyway. The only soldiers left were the drunk ones who had been singing: 'Ah, the sunshine of Mexico!' One of them, who was standing at the bar, a tall, fair-haired corporal, turned round and laughed at us again; as I remember, we were sitting there at our table, very quiet and well-behaved, hands on knees, the way we did during instruction period in barracks. The corporal then said something to the woman behind the bar and she brought us some clear schnapps in quite big glasses. 'We must drink to him now,' said Erich, nudging us with his knees, and I kept on calling 'Corporal!' until he realized I meant him; then Erich nudged us again and we stood up and shouted in unison: 'Prost, Corporal!' The other soldiers all roared with laughter, but the corporal raised his glass and called across to us: 'Prost, Grenadiers . . .'

The schnapps was sharp and bitter, but it warmed us, and we would have liked another.

The fair-haired corporal beckoned to Kurt, and Kurt went over to him and beckoned to us after a few words with the corporal. The corporal told us we were crazy not to have any money, we ought to sell something; and he asked us where we came from and where we were being sent, and we told him we were waiting at the barracks and were to be flown out to the Crimea. His face became serious, and he said nothing. Then I asked him what we could sell, and he said: anything.

We could flog anything here, he said, coats and caps, long underwear, watches, fountain pens.

We didn't want to sell our coats, we were too scared, it was against regulations, and besides we felt the cold very much, that time we were in Odessa. We emptied out our pockets: Kurt had a fountain pen, I had a watch, and Erich a brand-new leather wallet he had won at a lottery back at barracks. The corporal took all three and asked the woman what she would give for them; she examined everything very minutely, said it was poor stuff, and offered two hundred and fifty marks, a hundred and eighty for the watch alone.

The corporal said that wasn't much, two hundred and fifty, but he also told us she wouldn't be likely to offer more, and if we had to fly to the Crimea next day maybe it didn't make any difference, we might as well take it.

Two of the soldiers who had been singing: 'Ah, the sunshine of Mexico!' came over and tapped the corporal on the shoulder; he nodded to us and they all left together.

The woman had handed all the money to me, so I ordered for each of us two portions of roast pork on bread and a large schnapps, then we each had another two portions of roast pork and another schnapps. The meat was fresh and juicy, hot and almost sweet, the bread was soaked with fat, and we had another schnapps. Then the woman told us she had no more roast pork, only sausages, so we each had a sausage and ordered some beer to go with it, thick, dark beer, and we had another schnapps and ordered cakes, flat dry cakes made of ground nuts; then we had some more schnapps and were not drunk at all; we felt warm and snug and forgot all about our prickly long underwear and sweaters; and some more soldiers came in and we all sang: 'Ah, the sunshine of Mexico! . . .'

By six o'clock we had spent all our money, and still we weren't drunk; we went back to barracks because we had nothing else to sell. Along the dark, uneven road there were no more lights, and when we reached the gates the sentry told us to report to the guardhouse. The guardhouse was hot and dry, dirty, and smelled of tobacco, and the sergeant shouted at us and told us we needn't think we could get away with it. But that night we slept very well, and the next morning we again drove in the great rattling trucks along cobbled streets to the airfield, and it was cold there in

Odessa, the weather was gloriously clear, and at last we were boarded onto the planes; and as they rose into the sky we suddenly knew that we would never come back, never . . .

'Stranger, Bear Word
to the Spartans We...'

After the truck stopped the engine kept on throbbing for a while; somewhere outside a big gate was flung open. Light fell through the shattered window into the truck, and I saw that the lamp in the roof was smashed too; only its metal screw was left sticking out of the socket, with a few quivering wires and shreds of glass. Then the engine stopped, and outside a voice shouted: 'The dead over here – got any dead in there?'

'For Chrissake,' the driver called back, 'don't you bother about the blackout any more?'

'What the hell good is a blackout when the whole town's burning like a torch?' shouted the other voice. 'Well? Got any dead in there?'

'Dunno.'

'The dead over here, d'you hear? And the others up the stairs into the art room, right?'

'O.K., O.K.'

But I wasn't dead yet, I was one of the others, and they carried me up the stairs. First came a long, dimly lit corridor, green oil-paint on the walls; bent, black, old-fashioned clotheshooks had been let into the walls, and there were doors with little enamel plaques: VIa and VIb, and between these doors, shining softly under glass in a black frame, Feuerbach's Medea gazed into the distance; then came doors with Va and Vb, and between them hung a photograph of the boy plucking a thorn from his foot, its marvellous russet sheen framed in brown.

The great central column at the foot of the stairs was there too, and behind it, long and narrow, a beautiful plaster reproduction of the Parthenon frieze, creamy yellow, genuine, antique,

everything was all there just as it should be: the ancient
warrior, resplendent and formidable, plumed like a cock;
along the staircase wall – yellow oil-paint here – they
m the Hohenzollern rulers down to Hitler ...

here, in the narrow passageway, where at last I
on my stretcher for a few paces, there was t'~
est, most colourful picture of all: old Frederick the
Gre... ... his sky-blue uniform, lively eyes, and the great shining gold star on his chest.

Once again I was lying tilted on the stretcher and being carried
past the racial paradigms, including the Nordic captain with the
eagle eye and the stupid mouth, the Rhine maiden, a bit bony
and severe, the East Prussian with his broad grin and bulbous
nose, and the Alpine profile with lantern jaw and Adam's apple;
then came another corridor, again I lay level on my stretcher for
a few paces, and just before the stretcher-bearers swung round
onto the second staircase I caught a glimpse of it: the war
memorial surmounted by the great gilded Iron Cross and the
stone laurel wreath.

This all happened very quickly: I am not heavy, and the
stretcher-bearers were in a great hurry. Yet it might all be a
hallucination, I was running a high fever and my whole body
hurt – head, arms, and legs, and my heart was thumping like
crazy. You see a lot of funny things when you're feverish.

But after the Nordic faces came all the other things: the three
busts of Caesar, Cicero, and Marcus Aurelius, superb reproductions, standing sedately side by side against the wall, yellowed
and genuine, antique and dignified, and then as we swung round
the corner came the Hermes column, and way at the end of the
corridor – painted pink here – way, way at the end of the corridor
Zeus's big ugly mug hung over the entrance to the art room; but
that was still a long way off. To the right, through the window,
I could see fire reflected, the whole sky was red, and dense black
clouds of smoke filed past in solemn procession . . . And again
my eyes turned to the left and I saw the little plaques over the
doors, Ia and Ib, and between the musty brown doors I saw just

the tip of Nietzsche's nose and his moustache in a gilt frame because the other half of the picture had a sign stuck over it saying: 'Minor Surgery' . . .

I wonder, I thought fleetingly . . . I wonder . . . and there it was: the picture of Togoland, large, highly coloured, flat as an old engraving, a thing of beauty, and in the foreground in front of the colonial houses, in front of the Africans and the soldier standing pointlessly around with his rifle, in the very foreground was the huge, lifelike bunch of bananas: one bunch on the left, one on the right, and on the middle banana in the right-hand bunch something had been scribbled, I could just make it out. I must have written it myself . . .

But just at that moment the door to the art room was flung open, and I floated in under Zeus's whiskers and shut my eyes. I didn't want to see any more. The art room smelled of iodine, excrement, bandages, and tobacco, and it was noisy. As they set me down I asked the stretcher-bearers: 'Light me a cigarette, will you, top left-hand pocket.'

I could feel one of them fumbling in my pocket, a match hissed, and the lighted cigarette was stuck between my lips. I took a long pull. 'Thanks,' I said.

All this, I thought, doesn't prove a thing. Logically speaking, every high school has an art room, corridors with bent old clotheshooks let into green- and yellow-painted walls; logically speaking, the fact that Medea hangs between VIa and VIb and Nietzsche's moustache between Ia and Ib is no proof that I'm in my old school. No doubt there's some regulation requiring it to hang there. Rule for Prussian High Schools: Medea between VIa and VIb, Boy with a Thorn on that wall, Caesar, Marcus Aurelius, and Cicero in the corridor, and Nietzsche upstairs where they're already taking philosophy. Parthenon frieze, coloured print of Togoland. Boy with a Thorn and Parthenon frieze are, after all, good old stand-bys, traditional school props, and no doubt I wasn't the only boy who had been moved to write on a banana: Long live Togoland. And the jokes, too, that boys tell each other in school are always the same. Besides, maybe I'm feverish, maybe I'm dreaming.

The pain had gone now. In the truck it had still been pretty bad; I had yelled every time they drove through the small pot-holes, the shell craters had been better: the truck rose and sank like a ship in a wave-trough. But now the injection they had stuck in my arm somewhere in the dark seemed to be working: I had felt the needle boring through the skin and my leg lower down getting all hot.

It can't be true, I thought, the truck couldn't have driven that far: nearly twenty miles. Besides, I feel nothing: apart from my eyes, nothing tells me I'm in my school, in my old school that I left only three months ago. Eight years in the same school is a pretty long time – is it possible that after eight years only your eyes recognize the place?

Behind my closed lids I saw it all again, reeling off like a film: downstairs corridor, painted green, up the stairs, painted yellow, war memorial, corridor, up more stairs, Caesar, Cicero, Marcus Aurelius . . . Hermes, Nietzsche's moustache, Togoland, Zeus's ugly mug . . .

I spat out my cigarette and yelled: it always felt good to yell; but you had to yell loud, it was a glorious feeling, I yelled like mad. When someone bent over me I still didn't open my eyes; I smelled someone's breath, hot and fetid with tobacco and onions, and a quiet voice asked: 'What's the matter?'

'I want a drink,' I said, 'and another cigarette, top pocket.'

Once more someone fumbled in my pocket, once more a match hissed, and someone stuck a burning cigarette between my lips.

'Where are we?' I asked.

'In Bendorf.'

'Thanks,' I said, and drew on my cigarette.

So at least I really was in Bendorf, in my home town, that is, and unless I had an exceptionally high fever there seemed to be no doubt that I was in a high school with a classics department: it was certainly a school. Hadn't that voice downstairs shouted:

43

'The others in the art room'? I was one of the others, I was alive; the living were evidently the others. The art room was there, then, and if I could hear properly why shouldn't I be able to see properly, so it was probably true that I had recognized Caesar, Cicero, and Marcus Aurelius, and that could only happen in a classics high school; I didn't think they stood those fellows up against the wall in any other kind of school.

At last he brought me some water: again I smelled the tobacco and onion breath and, without wanting to, I opened my eyes: they saw a weary, elderly, unshaven face above a fireman's uniform, and an old man's voice whispered: 'Drink, lad!'

I drank; it was water, but water is glorious; I could taste the tin mug against my lips, and it was wonderful to feel how much water was still waiting to be drunk, but the fireman whisked the mug from my lips and went off: I yelled, but he didn't turn round, just gave a weary shrug of the shoulders and walked on; a man lying next to me said quietly: 'No use yelling, they haven't any more water. The town's burning, you can see for yourself.'

I could see it through the blackout curtains, there were flares and booms behind the black material, red behind black like in a stove when you throw on fresh coal. I could see it all right: the town was burning.

'What town is it?' I asked the man lying next to me.

'Bendorf,' he said.

'Thanks.'

I looked straight ahead at the row of windows and sometimes at the ceiling. The ceiling was still in perfect condition, white and smooth, with a narrow antique stucco border; but all schools have antique stucco borders on their art-room ceilings, at least the good old traditional classics high schools. No doubt about that.

I had to accept the fact that I was in the art room of a classics high school in Bendorf. Bendorf has three of these schools: Frederick the Great School, Albertus School, and – perhaps I need hardly add – the last, the third, was Adolf Hitler School. Hadn't old Frederick's picture on the staircase wall at Frederick

the Great School been the biggest, the most colourful and resplendent of all? I had gone to that school for eight years, but
why couldn't the same picture hang in exactly the same place in
other schools, so clear and noticeable that it couldn't fail to catch
your eye whenever you went up the first flight of stairs?

Outside I could hear the heavy artillery firing now. There was
hardly any other sound; just occasionally you could hear flames
consuming a house and somewhere in the dark a roof would cave
in. The artillery was firing quietly and regularly, and I thought:
Good old artillery! I know that's a terrible thing to think, but
I thought it. God, how reassuring the artillery was, how soothing:
dark and rugged, a gentle, almost refined organ sound, aristocratic somehow. To me there is something aristocratic about
artillery, even when it's firing. It sounds so dignified, just like war
in picture books . . . Then I thought of how many names there
would be on the war memorial when they reconsecrated it and
put an even bigger gilded Iron Cross on the top and an even
bigger stone laurel wreath, and suddenly I realized: if I really
was in my old school, my name would be on it too, engraved in
stone, and in the school year-book my name would be followed
by – 'went to the front straight from school and fell for . . .'

But I didn't know what for, and I didn't know yet whether I
was in my old school. I felt I absolutely had to make sure. There
had been nothing special about the war memorial, nothing unusual, it was like all the rest, a ready-made war memorial, in fact
they got them from some central supply house . . .

I looked round the art room, but they had removed the pictures,
and what can you tell from a few benches stacked up in a corner,
and from the high, narrow windows, all close together to let in a
lot of light because it was a studio? My heart told me nothing.
Wouldn't it have told me something if I had been in this place
before, where for eight years I had drawn vases and practised
lettering, slender, delicate, beautiful reproductions of Roman
vases that the art teacher set on a pedestal up front, and all kinds
of lettering, Round, Antique, Roman, Italic? I had loathed these
lessons more than anything else in school, for hours on end I had

45

suffered unutterable boredom, and I had never been any good at drawing vases or lettering. But where were my curses, where was my loathing, in the face of these dun-coloured, monotonous walls? No voice spoke within me, and I mutely shook my head.

Over and over again I had erased, sharpened my pencil, erased . . . nothing . . .

I didn't know exactly how I had been wounded. I only knew I couldn't move my arms or my right leg, just the left one a little; I figured they had bandaged my arms so tightly to my body that I couldn't move them.

I spat the second cigarette into the aisle between the straw pallets and tried to move my arms, but it was so painful I had to yell; I kept on yelling; each time I tried it, it felt wonderful to yell. Besides, I was mad at not being able to move my arms.

Suddenly the doctor was standing in front of me; he had taken off his glasses and was peering at me. He said nothing; behind him stood the fireman who had brought me the water. He whispered something into the doctor's ear, and the doctor put on his glasses: I could distinctly see his large grey eyes with the faintly quivering pupils behind the thick lenses. He looked at me for a long time, so long that I had to look away, and he said softly: 'Hold on, it'll be your turn in a minute . . .'

Then they picked up the man lying next to me and carried him behind the blackboard; my eyes followed them: they had taken the blackboard apart and set it up crossways and hung a sheet over the gap between wall and blackboard; a lamp was glaring behind it . . .

There was not a sound until the sheet was pushed aside and the man who had lain next to me was carried out; with tired impassive faces the stretcher-bearers carted him to the door.

I closed my eyes again and thought, I must find out how I've been wounded and whether I'm in my old school.

It all seemed so cold and remote, as if they had carried me through the museum of a city of the dead, through a world as irrelevant as it was unfamiliar, although my eyes, but only my eyes, recognized it; surely it couldn't be true that only three months ago I had sat in this room, drawn vases and practised lettering, gone downstairs during breaks with my jam sandwich, past Nietzsche, Hermes, Togoland, Caesar, Cicero, Marcus Aurelius, taking my time as I walked down to the lower corridor where Medea hung, then to the janitor, to Birgeler, for a glass of milk, milk in that dingy little room where you could risk a smoke although it was against the rules. They must be carrying the man who had lain next to me downstairs now, to where the dead were lying, maybe the dead were lying in Birgeler's grey little room that smelled of warm milk, dust, and Birgeler's cheap tobacco ...

At last the stretcher-bearers came back, and now they lifted me and carried me behind the blackboard. I was floating again, passing the door now, and as I floated past I could see that was right too: in the old days, when the school had been called St Thomas's, a cross had hung over the door, and then they had removed the cross, but a fresh, deep-yellow spot in the shape of a cross had stayed behind on the wall, hard and clear, more noticeable in a way than the fragile little old cross itself, the one they had removed; the outline of the cross remained distinct and beautiful on the faded wall. At the time they were so mad they repainted the whole wall, but it hadn't made any difference; the painter hadn't got quite the right colour: the cross stayed, deep yellow and clear, although the whole wall was pink. They had been furious, but it was no good: the cross stayed, deep yellow and clear on the pink wall; they must have used up their budget for paint so there wasn't a thing they could do about it. The cross was still there, and if you looked closely you could even make out a slanting line over the right arm of the cross where for years the boxwood sprig had been, the one Birgeler the janitor had stuck behind it, in the days when it was still permitted to hang crosses in schools ...

All this flashed through my mind during the brief second it took for me to be carried past the door to the place behind the blackboard where the glaring lamp shone.

I lay on the operating table and saw myself quite distinctly, but very small, dwarfed, up there in the clear glass of the light bulb, tiny and white, a narrow, gauze-coloured little bundle looking like an unusually diminutive embryo: so that was me up there.

The doctor turned away and stood beside a table sorting his instruments; the fireman, stocky and elderly, stood in front of the blackboard and smiled at me. His smile was tired and sad, and his unshaven, dirty face was the face of someone asleep. Beyond his shoulder, on the smudged reverse side of the blackboard, I saw something that, for the first time since being in this house of the dead, made me aware of my heart: somewhere in a secret chamber of my heart I experienced a profound and terrible shock, and my heart began to pound: the handwriting on the blackboard was mine. Up at the top, on the very top line. I know my handwriting: it is worse than catching sight of oneself in a mirror, much clearer, and there was not the slightest possibility of doubting the identity of my handwriting. All the rest hadn't proved a thing, neither Medea nor Nietzsche, neither the Alpine profile nor the banana from Togoland, not even the outline of the cross over the door: all that was the same in every school, but I don't believe they write on blackboards in other schools in my handwriting. It was still there, the Thermopylae inscription we had had to write, in that life of despair I had known only three months ago: Stranger, bear word to the Spartans we . . .

Oh I know, the board had been too short, and the art teacher had bawled me out for not spacing properly, for starting off with letters that were too big, and shaking his head he had written underneath, in letters the same size: Stranger, bear word to the Spartans we . . .

Seven times I had had to write it: in Antique, Gothic, Cursive, Roman, Italic, Script, and Round: seven times, plain for all to see: Stranger, bear word to the Spartans we . . .

The fireman, responding to a whispered summons from the doctor, had stepped aside, so now I saw the whole quotation, only slightly truncated because I had started off too big, had used up too many dots.

A prick in my left thigh made me jerk up, I tried to prop myself on my elbows, but couldn't. I looked down at my body, and then I saw: they had undone my bandages and I had no arms, no right leg, and I fell back instantly because I had no elbows to lean on. I screamed; the doctor and fireman looked at me in alarm, but the doctor merely shrugged his shoulders, keeping his thumb on the plunger of his hypo as he pressed it slowly and gently down. I tried to look at the blackboard again, but the fireman was standing right beside me now, obscuring it. He was holding down my shoulders, and I was conscious only of the scorched, grimy smell of his stained uniform, saw only his tired, sad face, and then recognized him: it was Birgeler.

'Milk,' I whispered . . .

Drinking in Petöcki

The soldier felt he was getting drunk at last. At the same moment it crossed his mind again, very clearly, that he hadn't a single pfennig in his pocket to pay the bill. His thoughts were as crystal-clear as his perception, he saw everything with the utmost clarity: the fat, short-sighted woman sitting in the shadows behind the bar, intent on her crocheting as she chatted quietly to a man with an unmistakably Magyar moustache – a true operetta-face, straight from the puszta, while the woman looked stolid and rather German, somewhat too respectable and sedate for the soldier's image of a Hungarian woman. The language they were chatting in was as unintelligible as it was throaty, as passionate as it was strange and beautiful. The room was filled with a dense green twilight from the many close-planted chestnut trees along the avenue leading to the station: a wonderful dense twilight that reminded him of absinthe and made the room exquisitely intimate and cosy. The man with the fabulous moustache, half-perched on a chair, looked relaxed and comfortable as he sprawled across the counter.

The soldier observed all this in great detail, at the same time aware that he would not have been able to walk to the counter without falling down. It'll have to settle a bit, he thought, then with a loud laugh shouted 'Hey there!', raised his glass towards the woman, and said in German: *'Bitte schön!'* The woman slowly got up from her chair, put aside her crochet work equally slowly, and, carrying the carafe, came over to him with a smile, while the Hungarian also turned round and eyed the medals on the soldier's chest. The woman waddling towards him was as broad as she was tall, her face was kind, and she looked as if she had heart trouble; clumsy pince-nez, attached to a worn black string, balanced on her nose. Her feet seemed to hurt too; while she filled his glass she took the weight off one foot and leaned with one hand on the table. She said something in her dark-toned Hungarian that was doubtless the equivalent of 'Prost' or 'Your very good health,' or perhaps even of some affectionate, motherly remark such as old women commonly bestow on soldiers.

The soldier lit a cigarette and drank deeply from his glass. Gradually the room began to revolve before his eyes; the fat proprietress hung somewhere at an angle in the air, the rusty old counter now stood on end, and the Hungarian, who was drinking sparingly, was cavorting about somewhere up near the ceiling like an acrobatic monkey. The next instant everything tilted the other way, the soldier gave a loud laugh, shouted 'Prost!', took another drink, then another, and lighted a fresh cigarette.

The door opened and in came another Hungarian, fat and short with a roguish, onion face and a few dark hairs on his upper lip. He let out a gusty sigh, tossed his cap onto a table, and hoisted himself onto a chair by the counter. The woman poured him some beer . . .

The gentle chatter of the three at the counter was wonderful, like a quiet humming at the edge of another world. The soldier took another gulp of wine, put down his empty glass, and everything resumed its proper place.

The soldier felt almost happy, he raised his glass again, repeating with a laugh '*Bitte schön!*'

The woman refilled his glass.

I've had almost ten glasses of wine, the soldier thought, I'll stop now, I'm so gloriously drunk that I feel almost happy. The green twilight thickened, the farther corners of the bar were already filled with impenetrable deep-blue shadows. What a crime, thought the soldier, that there are no lovers here. It would be a perfect spot for lovers, in this wonderful green and blue twilight. What a crime, he thought, as he pictured all those lovers somewhere out there in the world who had to sit around or chase around in the bright light, while here in the bar there was a place where they could talk, drink wine, and kiss . . .

Christ, thought the soldier, there ought to be music here now, and all these wonderful dark-green and dark-blue corners ought to be full of lovers – and I would sing a song. You bet I'd sing a song. I feel very happy, and I would sing those lovers a song, then I'd really quit thinking about the war, now I'm always thinking a little bit about this bloody war. Then I'd quit thinking about it altogether.

He looked closely at his watch: seven-thirty. He still had twenty minutes. He drank long and deep of the dry, cool wine, and it was almost as if someone had given him stronger spectacles: now everything looked closer and clearer and very solid, and he felt himself becoming gloriously, beautifully, almost totally drunk. Now he saw that the two men at the counter were poor, either labourers or shepherds, in threadbare trousers, and that their faces were tired and terribly submissive in spite of the dashing moustache and the wily onion look . . .

Christ, thought the soldier, how horrible it had been back there when I had to leave, so cold, and everything bright and full of snow, and we still had a few minutes left and nowhere was there a corner, a wonderful, dark, human corner where we could have kissed and embraced. Everything had been bright and cold . . .

'*Bitte schön!*' he shouted to the woman; then, as she approached, he looked at his watch: he still had ten minutes. When the woman started to fill his half-empty glass, he held his hand over it, shook his head with a smile, and rubbed thumb and forefinger together. 'Pay,' he said, 'how many pengös?'

He very slowly took off his jacket, slipped off the handsome grey turtleneck sweater, and laid it beside him on the table in front of the watch. The men at the counter had stopped talking and were looking at him, the woman also seemed startled. Very carefully she wrote a 14 on the table top. The soldier placed his hand on her fat, warm forearm, held up the sweater with the

other, and asked with a laugh: 'How much?' Rubbing thumb
and forefinger together again, he added: 'Pengös.'

The woman looked at him and shook her head, but he went on
shrugging his shoulders and indicating that he had no money
until she hesitantly picked up the sweater, turned it over, and
carefully examined it, even sniffed it. She wrinkled her nose a
little, then smiled and with a pencil quickly wrote a 30 next to
the 14. The soldier let go of her warm arm, nodded, raised his
glass, and took another drink.

As the woman went back to the counter and eagerly began
talking to the men in her throaty voice, the soldier simply opened
his mouth and sang; he sang: 'When the drum-roll sounds for
me' and suddenly realized he was singing well – singing well for
for the first time in his life; at the same time he realized he was
drunker again, that everything was gently swaying. He took
another look at his watch and saw he had three minutes in which
to sing and be happy, and he started another song: 'Innsbruck,
I must leave you.' Then with a smile he took the money the
woman had placed in front of him and put it in his pocket . . .

It was quite silent now in the bar, the two men with the
threadbare trousers and the tired faces had turned towards him,
and the woman had stopped on her way back to the counter and
was listening quietly and solemnly, like a child.

The soldier finished his wine, lighted another cigarette, and
knew he would walk unsteadily. But before he left he put some
money on the counter and, with a *'Bitte schön'*, pointed to the
two men. All three stared after him as he at last opened the door
and went out into the avenue of chestnut trees leading to the
station, the avenue that was full of exquisite, dark-green, dark-
blue shadows where a fellow could have put his arms around
his girl and kissed her good-bye . . .

Dear Old Renée

Whenever you turned up at her place around ten or eleven in the morning, she looked a real fat slattern. Her round massive shoulders bulged beneath the shapeless flowered smock, battered curlers were stuck in her lifeless hair like lead sinkers caught in muddy weeds; her face was bloated, and breadcrumbs still clung to the neckline of her smock. She made no attempt to conceal her unlovely morning appearance, for she was at home to only a few select customers – usually only me – whom she knew to be concerned less with her feminine charms than with her excellent drinks. And her drinks were excellent at that, and high-priced too; in those days she still had a very fine cognac. Besides, she gave credit. In the evening she was a real charmer: well-corseted, her shoulders and breasts high and firm, some sexy stuff sprayed on her hair and her eyes made up, scarcely a man could resist her, and perhaps I was one of the few she was willing to receive in the mornings just because she knew I was always able to withstand her charms in the evenings.

In the morning, around ten or eleven, she was a mess. Her disposition was bad then too, she was given to moralizing and to delivering herself of sententious utterances. When I knocked or rang (she preferred me to knock, 'It sounds so intimate,' she used to say), I would hear her shuffling footsteps, the curtain behind the frosted-glass door would be pushed aside, and I could see her shadow. She would peer through the pattern of flowers on the glass pane, muttering: 'Oh, it's you,' and push back the bolt.

She was truly a repulsive sight, but it was the only decent tavern in the place, with its thirty-seven grimy houses and two

54

run-down châteaux, and her drinks were first-rate; besides, she gave credit, and in addition to all this she was really very pleasant to talk to. And so the leaden morning hours would pass in no time. As a rule I stayed only until we could hear the distant voices of the company singing on its way back from drill, and it always gave you a funny feeling to hear the same old song, coming closer and closer, in the same old sluggish silence of that godforsaken hole.

'There it comes again,' was her invariable comment, 'that crappy war.'

And together we would watch the company, the first lieutenant, the sergeants, the corporals, the privates, all marching past the frosted-glass windowpane looking tired and dispirited; we would stand watching the company through the pattern of flowers. Between the roses and tulips were whole strips of clear glass, and you could see the lot of them, row after row, face after face, all sullen and hungry and apathetic ...

She knew nearly every one of them personally, in fact she knew them all. Even the teetotallers and the woman-haters, for it was the only decent tavern in the place, and even the most rabid ascetic sometimes has an urge to follow up a bowl of hot bad soup with a glass of lemonade, or in the evening possibly even a glass of wine, when he finds himself trapped in a godforsaken hole consisting of thirty-seven grimy houses and two run-down châteaux, a godforsaken hole that seems about to sink into the mud and to disintegrate in sloth and boredom ...

But our company wasn't the only one she knew; she knew all the first companies of all the battalions of the regiment, for, according to some intricately devised plan, after a certain length of time every first company of every battalion was sent back to this dreary place for a six-week period of 'rest and recuperation'.

During our second period of rest and recuperation, which we spent in drill and boredom, she was starting to deteriorate. She was losing her self-respect. She usually slept now till eleven, served beer and lemonade at noon in her dressing gown, closed up the place again in the afternoon, because, with the company out drilling, the village was as empty as a drained cesspool – and didn't open up again till around seven in the evening, after dozing away the afternoon. She had also stopped bothering about her income. She would lend money to anyone, have a drink with anyone, let her massive body be persuaded to dance, bawling out the songs and finally, with the approaching sound of taps, giving way to paroxysms of sobbing.

On our second arrival in the village I immediately reported sick. I had chosen a disease that made it imperative for the medic to allow me to go to Amiens or Paris to consult a specialist. I was in a pretty good mood as I knocked on her door around ten-thirty. There was not a sound in the village, the empty streets were deep in mud. Then came the familiar shuffling of her slippers, the rustle of the curtain, and Renée's muttered exclamation: 'Oh, it's you.' A smile flitted across her face. 'Oh, it's you!' she repeated as the door opened, 'You fellows back again?'

'That's right,' I said, throwing my cap onto a chair and following her. 'Bring me the best in the house, will you?'

'The best in the house?' she asked, looking somewhat at a loss.

She wiped her fingers on her smock. 'I'm sorry, I've been peeling potatoes.' She held out her hand; it was still small and firm, a pretty hand. I sat down on a bar stool after bolting the door from the inside.

She was standing rather undecidedly behind the bar.

'The best in the house?' she asked, at a loss.

'Yes,' I said, 'and make it snappy.'

'Hm,' she muttered, 'but it's a scandalous price.'

'Who cares, I've got money.'

'All right,' she said, wiping her hands again. The tip of her tongue appeared between her bloodless lips, a token of her painful dilemma.

'D'you mind if I bring my potatoes in here to peel?'

'Of course not,' I replied. 'Get a move on, and have a drink with me.'

When she had vanished beyond that narrow, scratched brown door to the kitchen, I looked round the room. Nothing had changed since last year. Over the bar hung the photograph of her alleged husband, a handsome marine with a black moustache, a colour photo showing the fellow framed in a lifebelt bearing the word '*Patrie*'. The fellow had cold eyes, a brutal chin, and a distinctly patriotic mouth. I didn't care for him. On either side hung a few pictures of flowers and lovers exchanging saccharine kisses. It was all exactly the same as a year ago. Possibly the furniture was a bit shabbier, but could it have got any shabbier? The bar stool I was perched on had one leg glued – I clearly recalled its being broken during a fight between Friedrich and Hans, a fight about an ugly girl called Lisette – and this leg still showed the depressing trickle of glue, like a runny nose, that someone had forgotten to rub off with sandpaper.

'Cherry brandy,' said Renée, a bottle in one hand and an enamel basin full of potatoes and peelings pinned to her side with her right arm.

'Any good?' I asked.

She smacked her lips. 'The best there is, love, a real good one.'

'Pour us a couple then, will you?'

She stood the bottle on the counter, let the basin slide onto a little stool behind the bar, and took two glasses from the shelf. Then she filled the shallow glasses with the red liquid.

'Prost, Renée,' I said.

'Prost, my lad!'

'Now then – what's new?'

'Nothing,' she sighed, deftly peeling her potatoes again. 'A few more skedaddled without paying, some glasses got smashed. That nice Jacqueline's having another baby and doesn't know whose it is. The rain's been raining and the sun's been shining, I'm an old woman now and I'm clearing out.'

'Clearing out, Renée?'

'Yes,' she said without emotion. 'Believe me, there's no fun in it any more. The boys have less and less money and get more and more cocky, drinks go down in quality and up in price. Prost, my lad!'

'Prost, Renée!'

We drank down the fiery red stuff, it was first-rate all right, and I immediately refilled our glasses.

'Prost!'

'Prost!'

'There,' she said finally, throwing the last peeled potato into a saucepan of water, 'that'll do for today. I'll just go and wash my hands so you don't have the smell of potatoes hanging around you. Potatoes smell horrible – don't you agree that potato peelings smell horrible?'

'Yes,' I said.

'You're a good lad.'

She vanished once more into the kitchen.

The cherry brandy was indeed excellent. A sweet fire of cherries flowed into me, and I forgot the lousy war.

'You like me better this way, eh?'

She was standing in the doorway, properly dressed now and wearing a cream-coloured blouse, and you could smell that she had washed her hands with good soap.

'Prost!' I said.

'Prost!'

'So you're really clearing out – but you're not serious?'

'I am,' she said, 'I'm dead serious.'

'Prost,' I said, and started to fill the glasses.

'No,' she said, 'if you don't mind I'll have a lemonade, it's a bit early for me.'

'All right, but go on.'

'Well,' she said, 'I've had it.' She looked at me, and in her eyes, those bleary, swollen eyes, there was a terrible fear. 'D'you hear, my lad? I've had it. It's driving me crazy, this silence. Just listen.' She gripped my arm so tightly that I was startled and really did listen. And it was uncanny: there wasn't a sound, and yet it wasn't silent either, there was an indescribable something in the air, a kind of bubbling: the sound of silence.

'D'you hear?' she asked, a note of triumph in her voice. 'It sounds like a dunghill.'

'A dunghill?' I said. 'Prost!'

'That's right,' she replied, swallowing some lemonade. 'It's exactly like a dunghill, that sound. I'm from the country, you know, from a little place up north near Dieppe, and lying in bed in the evening I used to hear that sound quite distinctly: it was silent, and yet not silent, and later I found out what it was: it's the dunghill, that queer snapping and bubbling and slurping and sucking you hear when people think there's silence. That's when the dunghill is working, dunghills work all the time, and that's exactly the sound they make. Listen!' She gripped my arm tightly again, gazing at me intently, imploringly, out of those bleary, swollen eyes . . .

But I refilled my glass and said: 'I see what you mean,' and although I knew just what she meant and could also hear that curious, seemingly illogical sound of bubbling silence, I wasn't scared the way she was; I felt protected, although it was pretty depressing to be sitting here in this lousy hole, in this lousy war, drinking cherry brandy with a panicky tavernkeeper at eleven in the morning.

'Ssh,' she said now, 'Listen.' Far away I could hear the rhythmic, monotonous singing of the company on its way back to the village.

But she put her hands over her ears.

'No,' she cried, 'not that! That's worse than anything. Every morning at the same minute that dreary singing, it's driving me crazy.'

'Prost,' I said with a laugh, filling my glass. 'Snap out of it!'

'No,' she cried again, 'that's why I want to leave, it's killing me!'

She kept her hands over her ears while I smiled at her, went on drinking, and followed the singing as it came closer and closer, and it was true, it did sound ominous in the silence of the village. Now the tramp of boots was clearly audible, the barking voices of the corporals in the intervals between singing, and the shouting of the lieutenant who always mustered enough courage and strength to call out: 'Come on, men, give us another song!'

'I can't take it any more,' whispered Renée, on the verge of tears from sheer exhaustion and still doggedly holding her hands over her ears, 'it's killing me, lying like this on the dunghill and listening to them singing . . .'

This time I stood alone by the window as they marched past, row after row, face after face, hungry and tired, an almost exalted grimness in their faces, yet still apathetic and sullen and somewhere in their eyes a spark of fear . . .

'Come on,' I said to Renée, when the last of them had marched by and the singing had died away. I took her hands away from her ears. 'Don't be so silly.'

'No,' she said obstinately, 'I'm not silly, I'm quitting, I'm going to open a movie house somewhere, in Dieppe or Abbeville.'

'And how about us, what's going to happen to us?'

'My niece is coming here,' she said, looking at me, 'a pretty young thing, she'll brighten up the place, I've made up my mind to hand it over to my niece.'

'When?' I asked.

'Tomorrow.'

'Not tomorrow?' I asked.

'Don't worry,' she laughed, 'I tell you, she's young and pretty. Look!' She took a photo out of the drawer, but the girl in the picture didn't appeal to me at all; she was young and pretty, but cold, and she had the self-same patriotic mouth as the man whose picture hung over the counter with his lifebelt . . .

'Prost,' I said sadly, 'tomorrow, then.'

'Prost,' she said, filling her own glass too.

The bottle was empty, and I felt as if I were rocking on the bar stool like a ship on the high seas, and yet my mind was clear.

'How much,' I said.

'Three hundred,' she said.

But as I was pulling out the bills she made a sudden gesture, saying, 'No, don't, for old times' sake. You're the only one I cared for at all. Spend it all when my niece comes, if you feel like it. Tomorrow.'

'Good-bye,' and she waved to me, and as I went out I saw her dipping her glasses into the chrome sink to rinse them, and I knew that the niece would never have such pretty hands, such small firm hands, as hers, for hands and mouth are almost the same, and it would be terrible if she had patriotic hands . . .

Children Are Civilians Too

'No, you can't,' said the sentry gruffly.

'Why?' I asked.

'Because it's against the rules.'

'Why is it against the rules?'

'Because it is, chum, that's what; patients aren't allowed outside.'

'But,' I said with pride, 'I'm one of the wounded.'

The sentry gave me a scornful look: 'I guess this is the first time you've been wounded, or you'd know that the wounded are patients too. Go on, get back in.'

But I persisted.

'Have a heart,' I said, 'I only want to buy cakes from that little girl.'

I pointed outside to where a pretty little Russian girl was standing in the whirling snow peddling cakes.

'Get back inside, I tell you!'

The snow was falling softly into the huge puddles on the black schoolyard, the little girl stood there patiently, calling out over and over again: 'Khakes ... khakes ...'

'My God,' I told the sentry, 'my mouth's watering, why don't you just let the child come inside?'

'Civilians aren't allowed inside.'

'Good God, man,' I said, 'the child's just a child.'

He gave me another scornful look. 'I suppose children aren't civilians, eh?'

It was intolerable, the empty, dark street was wrapped in powdery snow, and the child stood there all alone, calling out 'Khakes ...' although no one passed.

I started to walk out anyway, but the sentry grabbed me by the sleeve and shouted furiously: 'Get back, or I'll call the sergeant!'

'You're a bloody fool,' I snapped back at him.

'That's right,' said the sentry with satisfaction. 'Anyone who still has a sense of duty is considered a bloody fool by you fellows.'

I stood for another half minute in the whirling snow, watching the white flakes turn to mud; the whole schoolyard was full of puddles, and dotted about lay little white islands like icing sugar. Suddenly I saw the little girl wink at me and walk off in apparent unconcern down the street. I followed along the inner side of the wall.

'Damn it all,' I thought, 'am I really a patient?' And then I noticed a hole in the wall next to the urinal, and on the other side of the hole stood the little girl with the cakes. The sentry couldn't see us here. May the Führer bless your sense of duty, I thought.

The cakes looked marvellous: macaroons and cream slices, buttermilk twists and nut squares gleaming with oil. 'How much?' I asked the child.

She smiled, lifted the basket towards me, and said in her piping voice: 'Two marks fifty each.'

'All the same price?'

'Yes,' she nodded.

The snow fell on her fine blonde hair, powdering her with fleeting silver dust; her smile was utterly betwitching. The dismal street behind her was empty, and the world seemed dead . . .

I took a buttermilk twist and bit into it. It was delicious, there was marzipan in it. 'Aha,' I thought, 'that's why these cost as much as the others.'

The little girl was smiling.

'Good?' she asked. 'Good?'

I nodded. I didn't mind the cold, I had a thick bandage round my head that made me look very romantic. I tried a cream slice and let the delectable stuff melt slowly in my mouth. And again my mouth watered . . .

'Here, I whispered, 'I'll take the lot, how many are there?'

She began counting, carefully, with a delicate, rather dirty

63

little forefinger, while I devoured a nut square. It was very quiet, it seemed almost as if there were a soft, gentle weaving of snowflakes in the air. She counted very slowly, made one or two mistakes, and I stood there quite still eating two more cakes. Then she raised her eyes to me suddenly, at such a startling angle that her pupils slanted upwards and the whites of her eyes were the thin blue of skim milk. She twittered something at me in Russian, but I shrugged my shoulders with a smile, whereupon she bent down and with her dirty little finger wrote a 45 in the snow; I added my five, saying: 'Let me have the basket too, will you?'

She nodded, carefully handing me the basket through the hole, and I passed a couple of hundred-mark bills through to her. We had money to burn, the Russians were paying seven hundred marks for a coat, and for three months we had seen nothing but mud and blood, a few whores, and money.

'Come back tomorrow, O.K.?' I whispered, but she was no longer listening, quick as a wink she had slipped away, and when I stuck my head sadly through the gap in the wall she had vanished, and I saw only the silent Russian street, dismal and empty; the snow seemed to be gradually entombing the flat-roofed houses. I stood there for a long time, like a sad-eyed animal looking out through a fence, and it was only when I felt my neck getting stiff that I pulled my head back inside the prison.

And for the first time I noticed the revolting urinal stench from the corner, and all the nice little cakes were covered with a light sugar-icing of snow. With a sigh I picked up the basket and walked towards the building; I did not feel cold, I had that romantic-looking bandage round my head and could have stood for another hour in the snow. I left because I had to go some place. A fellow has to go some place, doesn't he? You can't stand around and let yourself be buried in snow. You have to go some place, even when you're wounded in a strange, black, very dark country . . .

What a Racket

The Half-woman, the 'Woman With No Lower Half', turned out to be one of the most delightful persons I had ever met. She was wearing a charming sombrero-type straw hat, for, like any other modest housewife, she was sitting in the sun on the little raised porch that had been attached to her trailer home. Below the porch her three children were playing a very original game known to them as 'The Neanderthals'. The two youngest, a boy and a girl, were obliged to be the Neanderthal couple, while the oldest, a fair-haired youngster of eight who during performances was the Fat Lady's son, took the part of the modern explorer who discovers the Neanderthal couple. Right at the moment he was doing his best to wrench his younger siblings' jawbones out of their sockets so he could take them back to his museum.

The Half-woman stamped several times on the porch floor on account of the frenzied screams that were threatening to stifle our budding conversation.

The oldest boy's head appeared above the low railing, which was adorned with red geraniums, and he asked crossly: 'Yes?'

'Stop that bullying,' said his mother, a suppressed amusement in her gentle grey eyes. 'Why don't you play Air-raid Shelter or Bombed Out?'

The boy grumbled something that sounded like 'Nuts!', disappeared below the railing, and shouted to the others: 'Fire! The whole house is on fire!' Unfortunately I was unable to follow the further course of the game known as Bombed Out, for the Half-woman was now eyeing me somewhat more closely. In the shade of her broad-brimmed hat, with the sun shining warm and red through it, she looked much too young to be the mother of three children and to fulfil the exacting demands, five times a day, of the role of Half-woman.

'You are . . .' she said.

'Nothing,' I said, 'nothing at all. Consider me nothing but a nothing . . .'

'You are,' she placidly continued, 'a former black-market operator, I suppose.'

'That's right,' I said.

She shrugged her shoulders. 'I can't really offer you anything. In any case, wherever we found a spot for you, you would have to work – work, do you know what I mean?'

'Ma'am,' I replied, 'possibly your idea of a black-market operator's life is a little on the rosy side. Speaking personally, I was, one might say, at the front.'

'What?' She stamped her foot again on the porch floor, the children having set up a rather protracted and demented howling. Once again the boy's head appeared above the railing.

'Well?' he asked curtly.

'Play Refugees now,' the woman said quietly. 'You must flee from the burning city, understand?'

The boy's head vanished again, and the woman asked me: 'What?'

Oh, she hadn't lost the thread, not she.

'Right at the front,' I said, 'I was right in the front lines. Is that your idea of an easy way to make a living?'

'At the corner?'

'Well, at the station, actually, you know where I mean?'

'I do. And now?'

'I'd like some kind of a job. I'm not lazy, I assure you, ma'am, I'm not lazy.'

'Excuse me,' she said. Turning her delicate profile towards me she called into the trailer: 'Carlino, isn't the water boiling yet?'

'Hang on,' called a bored voice. 'I'm just making the coffee.'

'Are you going to have some?'

'No.'

'Then bring two cups, if you don't mind. You'll have a cup, won't you?'

I nodded. 'And I'll invite you to a cigarette.'

The screams below the porch now became so piercing that any further conversation would have been impossible. The Half-woman leaned over the geranium box and called: 'You must run for your lives, hurry, hurry – the Russians have reached the village!'

'My husband,' she said, turning round, 'isn't here at the moment, but when it comes to hiring I can . . .'

We were interrupted by Carlino – a slightly built, taciturn, swarthy fellow wearing a hairnet – emerging with cups and coffee pot. He looked at me suspiciously.

'Why won't you join us?' The woman asked him as he turned abruptly away.

'Not thirsty,' he mumbled, disappearing inside the trailer.

'When it comes to hiring, I can act pretty well on my own. All the same, you would have to have some kind of skill. Nothing is nothing.'

'Perhaps, ma'am,' I said humbly, 'I could grease wheels or take down the tents, drive the tractor or be the Strong Man's knockabout.'

'Driving the tractor is out,' she said, 'and there's quite an art to greasing wheels.'

'Or operate the brakes,' I continued, 'on the gondola swings . . .'

She raised her eyebrows haughtily, for the first time giving me a slightly disdainful look. 'Operating the brakes,' she said coldly, 'is a science, and it wouldn't surprise me if you broke all the customers' necks. Carlino is our brakeman.'

'Or . . .' I was about to suggest diffidently, but a little dark-haired girl with a scar across her forehead came dashing up the half-dozen steps that put me in mind of a gangplank.

Throwing herself into her mother's lap she sobbed indignantly: 'I've got to die . . .'

'What?' asked the Half-woman, aghast.

'I'm supposed to be the little refugee who freezes to death, and Freddi wants to sell my shoes and everything . . .'

'Well,' said her mother, 'if you will insist on playing Refugees . . .'

'But why always me?' said the child. 'It's always me who has to die. I'm always the one who's got to die. When we play Bombs or War or Tightrope Walkers, it's always me that's got to die.'

'Tell Freddi he's got to die, tell him I said it's his turn to die now.' The little girl ran off.

'Or?' asked the Half-woman. Oh, she didn't lose the thread that easily, not she.

'Or straighten nails, peel potatoes, ladle out soup, anything you say,' I cried in despair, 'just give me a chance!'

She stubbed out her cigarette, poured us each another cup of coffee, and gave me a long, smiling look. Then she said: 'I'll give you a chance. You're good at figures, aren't you? You had to be, didn't you, in your former occupation, so' – she hesitated a second – 'I'll make you cashier.'

I had no words, I was literally speechless, I just got up and kissed her small hand. We said no more, it was very quiet, all we could hear was Carlino humming to himself inside the trailer, the way a man hums when he is shaving . . .

At the Bridge

They have patched up my legs and given me a job I can do sitting down: I count the people crossing the new bridge. They get such a kick out of it, documenting their efficiency with figures, that senseless nothing made up of a few numbers goes to their heads, and all day long, all day long, my soundless mouth ticks away like clockwork, piling number on number, just so I can present them each evening with the triumph of a figure.

They beam delightedly when I hand over the result of my day's labours, the higher the figure the broader their smiles, and they have every reason to hug themselves when they climb into bed, for many thousands of pedestrians cross their new bridge every day . . .

But their statistics are wrong. I am sorry, but they are wrong. I am an untrustworthy soul, although I have no trouble giving an impression of sterling integrity.

Secretly it gives me pleasure to do them out of one pedestrian every so often, and then again, when I feel sorry for them, to throw in a few extra. I hold their happiness in the palm of my hand. When I am mad at the world, when I have smoked all my cigarettes, I just give them the average, sometimes less than the average; and when my spirits soar, when I am in a good mood, I pour out my generosity in a five-digit number. It makes them so happy! They positively snatch the sheet from my hand, their eyes light up, and they pat me on the back. How blissfully ignorant they are! And then they start multiplying, dividing, working out percentages, God knows what all. They figure out how many people crossed the bridge per minute today, and how many will have crossed the bridge in ten years. They are in love with the future-perfect tense, the future-perfect is their speciality – and yet I can't help being sorry that the whole thing is a fallacy.

When my little sweetheart crosses the bridge – which she does twice a day – my heart simply stops beating. The tireless ticking of my heart just comes to a halt until she has turned into the avenue and disappeared. And all the people who pass by during that time don't get counted. Those two minutes are mine, all mine, and nobody is going to take them away from me. And when she returns every evening from her ice-cream parlour, when she walks along on the far side, past my soundless mouth which must count, count, then my heart stops beating again, and I don't resume counting until she is out of sight. And all those who are lucky enough to file past my unseeing eyes during those minutes will not be immortalized in statistics: shadow-men and shadow-women, creatures of no account, they are barred from the parade of future-perfect statistics.

Needless to say, I love her. But she hasn't the slightest idea, and I would rather she didn't find out. I don't want her to suspect what havoc she wreaks in all those calculations, I want her to walk serenely off to her ice-cream parlour, unsuspecting and innocent with her long brown hair and slender feet, and to get lots of tips. I love her. It must surely be obvious that I love her.

Not long ago they checked up on me. My mate, who sits across the street and has to count the cars, gave me plenty of warning, and that day I was a lynx-eyed devil. I counted like crazy, no speedometer could do better. The chief statistician, no less, posted himself across the street for an hour, and then compared his tally with mine. I was only one short. My little sweetheart had walked past, and as long as I live I won't allow that adorable child to be whisked off into the future-perfect tense, they're not going to take my little sweetheart and multiply her and divide her and turn her into a meaningless percentage. It made my heart bleed to have to go on counting without turning round to watch her, and I am certainly grateful to my mate across the street who had to count the cars. It might have cost me my job, my very existence.

The chief statistician clapped me on the shoulder and said I was a good fellow, trustworthy and loyal. 'To be out one in one hour,' he said, 'really makes no odds. We allow for a certain margin of error anyway. I'm going to apply for your transfer to horse-drawn vehicles.'

Horse-drawn vehicles are, of course, money for jam. There's nothing to it. There are never more than a couple of dozen horse-drawn vehicles a day, and to tick over the next number in your brain once every half hour – what a cinch!

Horse-drawn vehicles would be terrific. Between four and eight they are not allowed across the bridge at all, and I could walk to the ice-cream parlour, feast my eyes on her or maybe walk her part-way home, my little uncounted sweetheart . . .

Parting

We were in that bleak, miserable mood that comes when you have already said good-bye but can't part because the train hasn't left yet. The station was like all stations, dirty and draughty, filled to its vaulted roof with vapoury haze and noise, the noise of voices and railway coaches.

Charlotte was standing at the window of the long corridor, constantly jostled and shoved from behind, the object of much cursing, but during these final precious minutes, the last we would ever share, we needed more than just a wave from an overcrowded compartment...

'It was nice of you,' I said, for the third time, 'it really was nice of you to stop by on your way to the station.'

'Don't be absurd, look how long we've known each other. Fifteen years.'

'That's right, we're thirty now, still ... you needn't have.'

'Please—. Yes, we're thirty now. As old as the Russian revolution.'

'As old as dirt and hunger ...'

'A bit younger ...'

'You're right, we're terribly young.'

She laughed.

'Did you say something?' she asked nervously: she had been bumped from behind with a heavy suitcase.

'No, it was my leg.'

'You must do something about it.'

'Yes, I will do something about it, it really talks too much.'

'Is it all right for you to stand so long?'

'Yes ...' and what I really wanted to tell her was that I loved her, but I couldn't find the words, for fifteen years I hadn't been able to find the words.

'What was that?'

'Nothing – Sweden, so you're going to Sweden.'

'Yes, I feel a bit ashamed, this has become part of our life, really, the dirt and rags and ruins, and I feel a bit ashamed. I feel like a deserter ...'

'Nonsense, that's where you belong, be glad you're going to Sweden.'

'Sometimes I am glad, you know, the food, that must be marvellous, and no ruins, no ruins at all. His letters sound so enthusiastic ...'

The voice that always announces the train departures sounded out now one platform closer, and I held my breath, but it was not our platform. The voice was only announcing the arrival of an international train from Rotterdam to Basel, and as I looked at Charlotte's small, delicate face I suddenly recalled the smell of soap and coffee, and I felt utterly wretched.

For a moment a desperate courage filled me, I wanted to drag this little person out of the window and keep her here, for she was mine, I loved her ...

'What's the matter?'

'Nothing,' I said, 'be glad you're going to Sweden.'

'I am. His vitality is fantastic, don't you agree? A prisoner of war for three years in Russia, that hair-raising escape, and now he's in Sweden lecturing on Rubens.'

'Fantastic, it really is.'

'You must get busy too, get your degree at least ...'

'Oh shut up!'

'What?' she asked, horrified. 'What?' She had gone quite pale.

'Forgive me,' I whispered, 'I mean my leg, I talk to it sometimes ...'

She didn't look in the least like Rubens, she looked more like Picasso, and I kept wondering why on earth he had married her, she wasn't even pretty, and I loved her.

It was quieter now on the platform, everyone had got onto the train, a few people stood around seeing their friends off. Any moment now the voice would say the train was leaving. Any moment might be the last . . .

'You really must do something, anything, you can't go on like this.'

'No, I can't,' I said.

She was the very opposite of Rubens: slim, long-legged, high-strung, and she was as old as the Russian revolution, as old as the hunger and dirt in Europe, as old as the war.

'I can't believe it . . . Sweden . . . it's like a dream.'

'It is all a dream.'

'Do you think so?'

'Of course. Fifteen years. Thirty years . . . another thirty years. Why bother about a degree, it's not worth the effort. Be quiet, damn you!'

'Are you talking to your leg?'

'Yes.'

'What does it say?'

'Listen.'

We were quite silent, we looked at one another and smiled, and we told one another without saying a word.

She smiled at me: 'Do you understand now, is it all right?'

'Yes . . . yes.'

'Truly?'

'Yes, yes.'

'You see,' she went on softly, 'it's not important to be together, and all that. That's not what really matters, is it?'

The voice that announces the train departures was right above me now, official, distinct, and I winced, as if a great grey, impersonal whip had come swishing down under the vaulted roof.

'Good-bye!'

'Good-bye!'

Very slowly the train started to move, sliding away in the darkness under the great roof.

Breaking the News

Do you know those dreadful little places where you keep wondering why the railway ever built a station there; where infinity seems to have congealed over a handful of dirty houses and a dilapidated factory, with fields on all sides condemned to eternal sterility; where you are suddenly aware that they are without hope because there is not a tree, not even a steeple, in sight? The man with the red cap – at last, at last, he gives the signal for the train to pull out – vanishes beneath a signboard bearing an imposing name, and you feel he is paid just to sleep twelve hours a day under a blanket of boredom. A grey horizon is draped over bleak fields cultivated by no one.

Yet I was not the only person to get out; an old woman carrying a large brown-paper parcel stepped down from the next compartment, but by the time I had emerged from the grimy little station she had disappeared as if swallowed up by the ground, and for a moment I was at a loss, not knowing whom to ask for directions. The scattering of brick houses with their dead windows and yellowish-green curtains defied all idea of human habitation, and at right angles to this token street ran a black wall that seemed on the point of collapse. I walked towards this grim-looking wall, afraid to knock at one of the houses of the dead. Then I turned the corner, and next to the grubby, barely legible sign saying 'Inn', I read the words 'Main Road' in clear, neat white lettering on a blue ground. A few more houses forming a crooked façade, crumbling plaster, and on the opposite side, long and windowless, the dingy factory wall like a barricade to the land of desolation. Following my instinct I turned left, but here the place suddenly came to an end; the wall continued for another ten yards or so, then came a leaden-grey field with a barely visible shimmer of green; somewhere the field merged with the grey, limitless horizon, and I had the terrible feeling that I was standing at the end of the world on the brink of a bottomless abyss, as if condemned to be dragged down into that silent, sinister, irresistible undertow of utter hopelessness.

On my left was a small, squat cottage, the kind workmen build in their spare time; I swayed, stumbled, towards it. Passing through a pitiful little gate with a leafless briar rose growing above it, I saw the number, and knew I had come to the right house.

The faded green shutters, their paint long washed away by the rain, were firmly closed, as if glued tight; the low roof – I could reach the gutter with my hand – had been patched with rusty corrugated sheets. The silence was absolute: it was the hour when twilight pauses for breath before welling up, grey and inexorable, over the edge of the horizon. I hesitated for a moment or two at the front door, wishing I had died in '45 when . . . instead of standing here about to enter this house. Just as I was going to raise my hand to knock, I heard a cooing sound, a woman's laugh, from inside; that mysterious, indefinable laugh that, depending on our mood, can either soothe us or wring our hearts. Only a woman who was not alone could laugh like that: again I hesitated, and again the burning, rending desire rose up in me to plunge into the grey infinity of the falling twilight that now hung over the broad fields and was beckoning, beckoning me . . . and with my last ounce of strength I pounded on the door.

First silence, then whispers – and footsteps, soft, slippered footsteps; the door opened, and I saw a fair, pink-cheeked woman who immediately put me in mind of that kind of indescribable radiance that illumines the farthest corners of a shadowy Rembrandt. Golden-red she glowed like a lamp before my eyes in this eternity of grey and black.

With a low cry she stepped back, holding the door open with trembling hands, but when I had taken off my army cap and said, hoarsely, 'Good evening,' the rigid lines of fear slackened in that strangely shapeless face, and she smiled uneasily and said, 'Yes.' In the background a muscular male figure loomed up and melted into the obscurity of the narrow passage. 'I'd like to see Frau Brink,' I said in a low voice. 'Yes,' the woman repeated tonelessly, and nervously pushed open a door. The male figure disappeared in the gloom. I entered a small room, crammed with shabby furniture, where the odour of bad food and excellent cigars seemed to have settled permanently. Her white hand went up to the switch: now that the light fell on her she seemed pale and amorphous, almost corpselike, only her fair, reddish hair was alive and warm. Her hands still trembling, she clutched her dark-red dress to her heavy breasts although it was closely buttoned – almost as if she were afraid I might stab her. The look in her watery blue eyes was wary, alarmed, as if, certain that some terrible sentence was awaiting her, she were facing a judge. Even the cheap sentimental prints seemed to have been stuck on the walls like indictments.

'Don't be alarmed,' I said, my voice tense, and instantly I knew that was the worst way I could possibly have chosen to begin, but before I could go on she said, in a strangely composed voice: 'I know all about it, he's dead . . . dead.' I could only nod. I reached into my pocket to hand over his few belongings, but in the passage a furious voice shouted 'Gitta!' She looked at me in despair, then flung open the door and called out shrilly: 'For God's sake, can't you wait five minutes – ?' and banged the door shut again, and I could picture the man slinking off into a corner. Her eyes looked up defiantly, almost triumphantly, into mine.

I slowly placed the wedding ring, the watch, and the paybook with the well-thumbed photograph on the green plush table-cloth. Suddenly she started to sob, wild, terrible cries like an animal's. The outlines of her face dissolved, became soft and shapeless like a slug, and shining teardrops gushed out between her short fleshy fingers. She collapsed onto the sofa, leaning on the table with her right hand while with her left she fingered the pathetic little objects. Memory seemed to be lacerating her with a thousand swords. I knew then that the war would never be over, never, as long as somewhere a wound it had inflicted was still bleeding.

I threw aside everything – disgust, fear, and desolation – like a contemptible burden and placed my hand on the plump, heaving shoulder, and as she turned her astonished face towards me I saw for the first time a resemblance to that photo of a pretty, smiling girl that I had had to look at so many hundreds of times, in '45 when . . .

'Where was it – please sit down – on the Russian front?' I could see she was liable to burst into tears again at any moment.

'No, in the West, in the prisoner-of-war camp – there were more than a hundred thousand of us . . .'

'And when?' Her gaze was wide and alert and extraordinarily alive, her whole face tense and young – as if her life depended on my reply. 'In July '45,' I said quietly.

She seemed to reflect for a moment, then she smiled – a pure and innocent smile, and I guessed why she was smiling.

Suddenly I felt as if the house were threatening to collapse about my ears, and I got up. Without a word she opened the door, she wanted to hold it open for me but I waited obstinately until she had gone ahead; and when she gave me her pudgy little hand she said, with a dry sob: 'I knew it, I knew it, when I saw him off – it's almost three years ago now – when I saw him off at the station,' and then she added almost in a whisper: 'Don't despise me.'

I felt a spasm of pain at these words – good God, surely I didn't look like a judge? And before she could stop me I had kissed her small, soft hand: it was the first time in my life I had ever kissed a woman's hand.

Outside darkness had fallen and, as if still under the spell of fear, I paused for a moment by the closed door. Then I heard her sobbing inside, loud, wild sobs, she was leaning against the front door with only the thickness of the wood between us, and at that moment I did indeed long for the house to collapse about her and bury her.

Then, slowly and very, very carefully – for I was afraid of

sinking any moment into an abyss – I groped my way back to the station. Lights were twinkling in the houses of the dead, the tiny place seemed to have grown in all directions. I could even see small lamps beyond the black wall that seemed to be illuminating vast expanses of yard. Dusk had become dense and heavy, foggy, vaporous, and impenetrable.

In the draughty little waiting-room there was only an elderly couple standing close together, shivering, in one corner. I waited a long time, my hands in my pockets, my cap pulled down over my ears, for there was a cold draught blowing in from the tracks, and night was falling lower, lower, like an enormous weight.

'If only there were a little more bread, and a bit of tobacco,' muttered the man behind me. And I kept leaning forward to peer along the parallel lines of tracks as they converged in the distance between dim lights.

Suddenly the door was flung open, and the man with the red cap, his face a picture of eager devotion to duty, shouted out, as if he had to make his voice carry across the waiting-room of a great railway station: 'Train for Cologne – ninety-five minutes late!'

At that moment I felt as if I had been taken prisoner for the rest of my life.

Between Trains in X

As I awoke, I was filled with a sense of almost utter isolation; I seemed to be floating in darkness on sluggish waters, borne along by aimless currents. Like a corpse that is finally washed up by the waves to the pitiless surface, I eddied this way and that, gently swaying in a dark void. I could not feel my limbs, they had ceased to be a part of me, and my senses no longer functioned. There was nothing to see, nothing to hear, no smell to cling to; only the soft touch of the pillow under my head linked me with reality, my head was the only thing I was conscious of. My thoughts were crystal-clear, barely dimmed by the racking headache that comes from bad wine.

Not even her breath was audible; she slept as lightly as a child, and yet I knew she must be lying beside me. There would have been no point in reaching out my hands to grope for her face or her soft hair, I had no hands; memory was but a memory of the mind, a bloodless structure that had left no trace on my body.

This was how I had often felt as I walked along the brink of reality with the assurance of the drunk making his way beside the narrow edge of a precipice, lurching with an unaccountable sense of balance towards a goal whose splendour is written on his mouth. I had walked along avenues lighted only by sparse grey lamps, leaden lamps that seemed only to suggest reality the better to be able to deny it. With unseeing eyes I had submerged myself in sombre streets crowded with people, knowing that I was alone, alone.

Alone with my head, and not even my whole head; nose, eyes, and ears were dead. Alone with only a brain that was straining to recapture memory, as a child builds apparently meaningless objects out of apparently meaningless sticks.

She must be lying beside me, although I had no physical consciousness of her.

The previous day I had left the train that continued south towards the Balkans as far as Athens while I had to change at this little station and wait for a train that was to take me closer to the Carpathian passes. As I stumbled across the platform, uncertain even of the name of the station, a drunken soldier came reeling towards me, a lone figure in his grey uniform among the Hungarians in their coloured civilian clothes. He was shouting insults that burned themselves into my brain like the slap in the face whose stinging pain one remembers all one's life.

'Bunch of whores!' he shouted. 'Swine, trash – I'm sick of the whole pack!' He was shouting all this into the very faces of the foolishly smiling Hungarians, while, carrying his heavy pack, he headed for the train I had just left.

Immediately a sinister steel-helmeted head called out from a train window: 'Hey you! You there!' The drunk drew his pistol, aimed at the steel helmet, people screamed, I made a dash for the soldier, put my arms around him, removed his weapon and hid it, keeping a firm grip on his flailing arms. The steel helmet shouted, people shouted, the drunk shouted, but the train moved off, and in most cases a moving train renders even a steel helmet powerless. I let go of the drunk, gave him back his pistol, and steered the dazed man to the exit.

The little place had a desolate look. The bystanders had quickly dispersed, the station square was empty, a tired and dirty railway employee directed us to a tiny bar beneath some low trees on the other side of the dusty square.

We put down our packs, and I ordered wine, that bad wine which was responsible for my present misery. The soldier sat there mute and angry. I offered him cigarettes, we smoked, and I had a good look at him: he was wearing the usual decorations, he was young, about my age, his fair hair hanging loosely over a flat, broad forehead into dark eyes.

'The point is, chum,' he said suddenly, 'I'm sick of the whole business, see?'

I nodded.

'Sick to death of it, see? I'm getting out.'

I looked at him.

'That's right,' he said soberly, 'I'm getting out, I'm heading for the puszta. I can handle horses, make a decent soup if I have to, they can lick my arse for all I care. Want to come along?'

I shook my head.

'Scared, eh? . . . No? . . . O.K., anyway I'm getting out. So long.'

He got up, left his pack on the floor, put some money on the table, nodded to me again, and went out.

I waited a long time. I didn't believe he had really quit, was really heading for the puszta. I kept an eye on his pack and waited, drank the bad wine and tried without success to strike up a conversation with the landlord, and stared at the square, across which, from time to time, wreathed in clouds of dust, dashed a cart drawn by thin horses.

After a while I had a steak, went on drinking the bad wine, and smoked cigars. The light was beginning to fade, now and then a cloud of dust would be wafted into the room through the open door, the landlord yawned or chatted with Hungarians as they drank their wine.

Darkness was coming on quickly, I shall never know all the things I was thinking about as I sat there and waited, drank wine, ate steak, watched the fat landlord, stared at the square, and puffed cigars . . .

My brain reproduced all this quite neutrally, spewing it out while I floated giddily around on those dark waters, in that hourless night, in a house I did not know, in a nameless street, beside a girl whose face I had never seen properly . . .

Later on I had hurried across to the station, found my train gone and the next one not due till the morning. I had paid my bill, left my pack lying beside the other one, and staggered out into the twilight of the little town. Grey, dark grey, flooded in on me from all sides, and only the sparse lamps gave the faces of passers-by the look of living people.

Somewhere I drank a better wine, looked forlornly into the unsmiling face of a woman behind the bar, smelled something like vinegar through a kitchen door, paid, and disappeared again in the dusk.

This life, I thought, is not my life. I have to behave as if this were my life, but I'm no good at it. It was quite dark by now, and the mild sky of a summer evening hung over the town. Somewhere the war was going on, invisible, inaudible in these silent streets, where the low houses slept beside low trees, somewhere in this absolute silence the war was going on. I was alone in this town, these people were not my people, these little trees had been unpacked from a box of toys and glued onto these soft grey sidewalks, with the sky hovering overhead like a soundless dirigible that was about to crash ...

Somewhere under a tree there was a face, faintly lighted from within. Sad eyes under soft hair that must be light brown although it looked grey in the night; a pale skin with a round mouth that must be red although it too looked grey in the night.

'Come along,' I said to the face.

I took hold of her arm, a human arm, the palms of our hands clung together, our fingers met and interlocked as we walked along in this unknown town and turned into an unknown street.

'Don't turn the light on,' I said as we entered the room I was now lying in, floating unattached in the darkness.

I had felt a weeping face in the dark and plunged into abysses, down into abysses the way you tumble down a staircase, a dizzying staircase of velvet; on and on I plunged, down one abyss after another ...

My memory told me all this had happened, and that I was now lying on this pillow, in this room, beside this girl, without being able to hear her breath; she sleeps as lightly as a child. My God, was my brain all that was left of me?

Often the pitch-black waters would seem to stand still, and

hope would stir in me that I was going to wake up, feel my legs, hear again, smell, and not merely think; and even this modest hope was a lot, for it would gradually subside, the pitch-black waters would start eddying again, repossess my helpless corpse and let it drift, timelessly, in total isolation.

My memory also told me that the night could not last forever. Day had to come some time. And it told me that I could drink, kiss, and weep, even pray, although you can't pray just with your brain. While I knew that I was awake, was lying awake in a Hungarian girl's bed, on her soft pillow in a dark, dark night, while I knew all this I could not help also believing that I was dead . . .

It was like a dawn that comes very gently and slowly, so indescribably slowly as to be barely perceptible. First you think you're mistaken; when you're standing in a foxhole on a dark night you can't believe that that's really the dawn, that soft, soft pale strip beyond the invisible horizon; you think you must be mistaken, your tired eyes are oversensitive and are probably reflecting something from some secret reserves of light. But it actually is the dawn, growing stronger now. It actually is getting light, lighter, daylight is growing stronger, the grey patch out there beyond the horizon is slowly spreading, and now you know for certain: day has come.

I suddenly realized I was cold; my feet had slipped out of the blanket, bare and cold, and the sense of chill was real. I sighed deeply, could feel my own breath as it touched my chin; I leaned over, groped for the blanket, covered my feet. I had hands again, I had feet again, and I could feel my own breath.

Then I reached down over the precipice to my left, fished up my trousers from the floor, and heard the sound of the match-box in the pocket.

'Don't turn on the light, please,' said her voice next to me now, and she sighed too.

'Cigarette?' I whispered.

'Yes,' she said.

In the light of the match she was all yellow. A dark yellow

mouth, round, black, anxious eyes, skin like fine, soft, yellow sand, and hair like dark honey.

It was hard to talk, to find something to say. We could both hear time trickling away, a wonderful dark flowing sound that swallowed up the seconds.

'What are you thinking about?' she asked all of a sudden. It was if she had fired a shot, quietly and with such perfect accuracy that a dam burst inside me, and before I had time to take another look at her face in the light of the glowing cigarette tips I found myself speaking. 'I was just thinking about who will be lying in this room seventy years from now, who will be sitting or lying on these six square feet of space, and how much he will know about you and me. Nothing,' I went on, 'he'll only know there was a war.'

We each threw our cigarette ends onto the floor to the left of the bed; they fell soundlessly onto my trousers. I shook them off, and the two little glimmering dots lay side by side.

'And then I was thinking who had been here seventy years ago, or what. Maybe there was a field, maybe corn or onions grew here, six feet over my head, with the wind blowing across, and every morning this sad dawn came up over the horizon of the puszta. Or maybe there was already a house belonging to someone.'

'Yes,' she said softly, 'seventy years ago there was a house here.'

I was silent.

'Yes,' she said, 'I think it was seventy years ago that my grandfather built this house. That's when they must have put the railway through here, he worked for the railway and built this little house with his savings. And then he went to war, ages ago, you know, in 1914, and he was killed in Russia. And then there was my father, he had some land and also worked for the railway; he died during this war.'

'Killed?'

'No, he died. My mother had died before. And now my brother lives here with his wife and children. And seventy years from now my brother's great-grandsons will be living here.'

'Maybe so,' I said, 'but they'll know nothing about you and me.'

'No, not a soul will ever know that you were here with me.'

I took hold of her small hand, it was soft, so soft, and held it close to my face.

In the square patch of window a dark-grey darkness showed now, lighter than the blackness of the night.

I suddenly felt her moving past me, without touching me, and I could hear the light tread of her bare feet on the floor; then I heard her dressing. Her movements and the sounds were so light; only when she reached behind her to do up the buttons of her blouse did I hear her breath come more strongly.

'You'd better get dressed,' she said.

'Let me just lie here,' I said.

'I don't want to put on the light.'

'Don't put on the light, let me just lie here.'

'But you must have something to eat before you go.'

'I'm not going.'

I could hear her pause as she put on her shoes and knew she was staring in astonishment into the darkness where I was lying.

'I see,' was all she said, softly, and I couldn't tell whether she was surprised or alarmed.

When I turned my head to one side I could see her figure outlined in the dark-grey dawn light. She moved very quietly about the room, found kindling and paper, and took the box of matches from my trouser pocket.

These sounds reached me almost like the thin, anxious cries of a person standing on a river bank and calling out to someone who is being driven by the current into a great body of water; and I knew then that if I did not get up, did not decide within the next minute or so to leave this gently heaving ship of isolation, I would die in this bed as if paralyzed, or be shot to death here on this pillow by the tireless myrmidons whose eyes miss nothing.

While I listened to her humming as she stood there by the stove gazing at the fire, its warm light growing with quiet wingbeats, I felt divided from her by more than a world. There she stood, somewhere on the periphery of my life, quietly humming and enjoying the growing fire; I understood all that, I could see it, smell the singeing of scorched paper, and yet nowhere could she have been further removed from me.

'Please get up, will you?' said the girl from across the room. 'You must leave now.' I heard her put a saucepan on the fire and began to stir; it was a soothing sound, the gentle scraping of the wooden spoon, and the smell of browning flour filled the room.

I could see everything now. The room was very small. I was lying on a low wooden bed, next to it a closet, brown, quite plain, that took up the whole wall as far as the door. Somewhere behind me there must be a table, chairs, and the little stove by the window. It was very quiet, and the early light still so opaque that it lay like shadows in the room.

'Please,' she said in a low voice, 'I have to go now.'

'You have to go?'

'Yes, I have to go to work, and first you must leave, with me.'

'Work?' I asked, 'why?'

'What a thing to ask!'

'But where?'

'On the railway tracks.'

'Railway tracks?' I asked. 'What do you do there?'

'We shovel stones and gravel so that nothing will happen to the trains.'

'Nothing's going to happen to the trains,' I said. 'Where do you work? Towards Nagyvárad?'

'No, towards Szegedin.'

'That's good.'

'Why?'

'Because then I won't have to pass you in the train.'

She laughed softly. 'So you're going to get up after all.'

'Yes,' I said. I shut my eyes again and let myself drop back into that swaying void whose breath was without smell and without trace, whose gentle rippling touched me like a quiet, barely perceptible waft of air; then I opened my eyes with a sigh and reached for my trousers, now lying neatly beside the bed on a chair.

'Yes,' I repeated, and got out of bed.

She stood with her back to me while I went through the familiar motions, drew on my trousers, did up my shoes, and pulled on my grey tunic.

I stood there for a while, saying nothing, my cigarette cold between my lips, looking at her figure, small and slight and now outlined clearly against the window. Her hair was beautiful, soft as a quiet flame.

She turned round and smiled. 'What are you thinking about now?' she asked.

For the first time I looked into her face: it was so simple that I could not take it in: round eyes, in which fear was fear, joy was joy.

'What are you thinking about now?' she asked again, and this time she was not smiling.

'Nothing,' I said. 'I can't think at all. I must go. There's no escape.'

'Yes,' she said and nodded. 'You must go. There's no escape.'

'And you must stay.'

'I must stay,' she said.

'You have to shovel stones and gravel so that nothing will happen and the trains can safely go where things do happen.'

'Yes,' she said, 'that's what I have to do.'

We walked down a silent street leading to the station. All streets lead to stations, and from stations you go off to war. We stepped aside into a doorway and kissed, and I could feel, as my hands lay on her shoulders, I could feel as I stood there that she was mine. And she walked away with drooping shoulders without once looking round at me.

She is all alone in this town, and although my way lies along the same street, to the station, I cannot go with her. I must wait till she has disappeared round that corner, beyond the last tree in this little avenue now lying remorselessly in full daylight. I must wait, I can only follow her at a distance, and I shall never see her again. I have to catch that train, go off to that war . . .

I have no pack now as I walk to the station, all I have is my hands in my pockets and my last cigarette between my lips, and that I shall soon spit out; but it is easier to be carrying nothing when you are once more walking slowly but unsteadily towards the edge of an abyss over which, at a given second, you are going to plunge, down to where we shall meet again. . .

And it was comforting when the train pulled in on time, cheerfully puffing steam between tall heads of corn and pungent tomato plants.

Reunion with Drüng

The burning pain in my head let me pass smoothly into the reality of time and space from a dream in which dark figures in grey-green coats had been pounding my skull with hard fists: I was lying in a low room in a farmhouse, and the ceiling seemed to be sinking down on me out of the green dimness like the lid of a tomb. The few traces of light that made the room barely discernible were green: a soft, yellow-frosted green with a black door sharply outlined by a bright band of light, a steadily deepening green that became the colour of old moss in the shadows above my face.

I awoke fully as a sudden, strangling nausea made me jerk upright, lean over, and vomit onto the invisible floor. The contents of my stomach seemed to drop into unplumbed depths, a bottomless well, before eventually penetrating my senses as liquid splashing on wood. I vomited again, bent painfully over the edge of the stretcher, and as I leaned back in relief the connection with the past became so clear that I at once remembered a roll of lemon drops, left over from last night's rations, that must still be in one of my pockets. My grimy fingers groped around in my greatcoat pockets, let a few loose cartridges fall clattering into the green abyss, and turned over every item: a packet of cigarettes, pipe, matches, handkerchief, a crumpled letter, and when I couldn't find what I was looking for in my coat pockets I undid my belt, the buckle clanking as it struck the iron stretcher bar. I found the roll at last in one of my trouser pockets, ripped off the paper, and stuck one of the tart-flavoured drops into my mouth.

At certain moments, when the pain flooded every level of my consciousness, relationships between time, space, and events would become confused again: the abyss on either side seemed to fall still further away, and the stretcher I was suspended on felt like a towering pedestal rising closer and closer towards the green ceiling. There were moments when I even thought I was dead, relegated to an agonizing limbo of uncertainty, and the door – outlined by its bright band – was like a gateway to light and enlightenment that some kindly hand must surely open; for at such moments I lay motionless as a statue, dead, and the only living thing was the burning pain spreading out from the wound in my head and associated with a sickening, all-pervading nausea.

Then the pain would ebb away again, as if someone were loosening a vice, and reality would become less brutal: the various shades of green were balm to my tormented eyes, the absolute silence soothing to my racked ears, and memory unwound within me like a roll of film in which I played no part. Everything seemed to lie in an infinitely remote past, whereas in fact not more than an hour could have gone by.

I tried to revive memories from my childhood, days spent in deserted parks instead of school, and these experiences seemed closer, and to involve me more directly, than what had happened an hour ago, although the pain in my head derived from these recent events and should have made me feel otherwise.

What had happened an hour ago I was now able to see very clearly, but distantly, as if I were looking from the edge of our globe into another world divided from ours by a vast abyss of glassy clarity. There I saw someone, who must be me, creeping over churned earth in nocturnal darkness, the lonely silhouette at intervals starkly illuminated by a distant tracer bullet. I watched this stranger, who must be me, struggling on visibly sore feet over the broken ground, often on all fours, then on his feet again, then back on all fours, up on his feet again, and finally heading for a dark valley where a group of similar dark figures stood gathered round a vehicle. In this spectral corner of the globe, where all was anguish and darkness, the stranger mutely took his place in a line of men whose mugs were being filled from metal cauldrons with coffee or soup by someone they did not know, had never seen, someone hidden by dense shadows, wordlessly ladling; the owner of a scared voice, also invisible, doled out bread, cigarettes, sausage, and candies into the waiting hands. And suddenly this mute, sombre spectacle on the valley floor was luridly lit up by a red flame followed by screams, whimpering, and the terrified neighing of a wounded horse; more dusky red flames kept shooting up out of the ground, stench and noise filled the air, then the horse screamed, I heard it pull away and dash off dragging the clattering field kitchen; and a fresh burst of fierce fire covered the figure that must be me.

And now here I was, lying on my stretcher, looking at the deepening shades of green in the dimness of this Russian farmhouse room where the only brightness was the light outlining the oblong of the door.

Meanwhile the nausea had subsided, the lemon drop had spread soothingly through the horrible muck filling my mouth; the vice of pain attacked less and less often, and I dug into my greatcoat pocket, pulled out cigarettes and matches, and struck a light. The flare revealed dark, damp walls, lit here and there by the flickering sulphur-yellow flame, and as I tossed aside the dying match I saw for the first time that I was not alone.

I saw beside me the grey, green-stained folds of a carelessly drawn-up blanket, saw the peak of a cap like an intense black shadow over a pale face, and the match went out.

At the same moment it occurred to me that there was nothing wrong with my hands or feet, so I kicked my blanket aside, sat up, and was startled to see how close I was to the ground: that apparently bottomless pit was scarcely more than knee-deep. I struck another match: my neighbour lay motionless, his face the colour of crepuscular light filtering through thin green glass, but before I could get any closer to have a good look at his face under the shadow of his cap, the match went out again, and I remembered that in one of my pockets there must still be a candle end.

The vice of pain made another assault, and I just managed to stagger to the edge of my stretcher in the dark. I sat down, dropping my cigarette onto the floor, and since I now had my back to the door I could see only darkness, a green opaque darkness containing just enough shadows to give me the feeling it was revolving, while the pain in my head seemed to be the motor making it revolve; the more the pain in my head swelled, the more violently did these darknesses revolve like separate discs overlapping as they revolved, until once more everything came to a standstill.

As soon as the attack was over I fingered my bandage: my head felt bulky and swollen; there was the hard, lumpy crust of clotted blood, and the ultrasensitive spot where the splinter must be. I knew now that the stranger over there was dead. There is a kind of silence and muteness going beyond sleep or unconsciousness, something infinitely icy, hostile, contemptuous, that in the darkness seemed doubly malevolent.

I finally found the candle end and lighted it. The glow was yellow and soft, it seemed to spread slowly and diffidently before unfolding its flame to its utmost limits, and when the candle had achieved its full radius I saw the beaten earth floor, the bluish whitewashed walls, a bench, and the dead stove with a pile of ashes lying in front of its sagging door.

I stuck the candle onto the edge of my stretcher so that the centre of its radiance fell on the dead man's face. I was not surprised to see Drüng. Rather I was surprised at my own lack of surprise, for it should have been a great shock: I had not seen Drüng for five years, and even then so briefly that we had exchanged only the barest civilities. We had been classmates for nine years, but there had been such a deep antipathy – not antimosity, merely indifference – between us that during those nine years we had spoken to each other for a total of scarcely an hour.

It was so unmistakably Drüng's spare face, his pointed nose, thrusting upward now, still and greenish, from the spare flatness of his face, his narrow-lidded eyes, always somewhat protruding, now closed by a stranger's hand; so unquestionably was it Drüng's face that there was really no need for me to confirm it by bending down and reaching in under the blanket folds for the label tied with string to one of his greatcoat buttons. On it I read by candlelight: Drüng, Hubert, Corporal, the number of his regiment, and under the heading 'Type of Injury': Multiple shell splinters, abdomen. Under this an academic hand had scrawled the word: Deceased.

So Drüng was really dead, or would I ever have doubted the hasty scrawl of an academic hand? Again I read the number of his regiment, one I had never heard of; then I took off Drüng's cap, whose black, sardonic shadow gave his face a cruel look, and there was that fairish, lacklustre hair which at various times during those fluctuating nine years had been right in front of me.

I was sitting quite close to the candle as its flickering glow swung round the room, the strongest core of its yellow flame always centred on Drüng's face as its feebler offshoots roamed ceiling, walls, and floor. I was sitting so close to Drüng that my breath brushed the ashen skin on which a stubble of beard proliferated, unsightly and reddish-brown, and suddenly for the first time I saw Drüng's mouth. During our daily encounters over so many years, the rest of his appearance had become so familiar that I would have recognized him in a crowd – although probably unconsciously – but now I realized I had never really looked at his mouth; it was as if I had never seen it before: fine-drawn, narrow-lipped, pain still clung to its pinched corners, a pain so alive that I thought I must be mistaken. This mouth seemed, even now, to be still fighting back the pent-up cries of pain to keep them from gushing out in a red spurt that would drown the world.

Beside me flickered the warm breath of the candle as it flared up, died down, then slowly fanned out, over and over again. I was looking at Drüng's face now without seeing him. I saw him alive, a sickly, shy fourth grader, heavy satchel on thin shoulders, shivering as he waited for the school doors to open. Then he would rush past the burly janitor and, still wearing his overcoat, plant himself beside the stove, standing guard over it with a defensive look in his eyes. Drüng had always felt the cold, he was of poor physique, poor in every way, the son of a widow whose husband had been killed in the war. He had been ten at the time, and he stayed like that, for nine years, shivering, of poor physique, poor in every way, the son of a widow whose husband had been killed in the war. Never once did he have time for those foolish things that memory alone makes memorable, while we often look back on humourless obsession with duty as a foolish thing; never once did he talk back to the teacher, for nine years he remained well-behaved, hard-working, always 'of average ability'. At fourteen he developed acne, at sixteen his skin was smooth again, at eighteen he had acne again, and he always felt the cold, even in summer, for he was of poor physique, poor in every way, the son of a widow whose husband had been killed in the war. He had a few friends, also of average ability, with whom he worked hard and was well-behaved; I hardly ever spoke to him, or he to me, and occasionally, as is to be expected over a period of nine years, he had sat in front of me, his lack-lustre, fairish hair had been in front of me, quite close, and he had always prompted me – now for the first time I realized he had always prompted me, faithfully and reliably, and when he didn't know the answer he had his own special way of obstinately shrugging his shoulders.

I had been crying for some time, and the candle was now casting its wider light around the room, sighing gently so that the barren little room seemed to rock like the cabin of a ship on the high seas. For some time – without being conscious of it – I had felt the tears running down my face, warm and soothing on my cheeks, and lower down, on my chin, cold drops that I automatically wiped away with my hand like a tearful child. But now that I remembered how he had always loyally prompted me, with never a word of thanks, faithfully and reliably, with none of the spitefulness of others who put too high a price on their knowledge to give it away – now I sobbed aloud, and the tears dripped through my matted beard into my muddy fingers.

And then I remembered about Drüng's father; during history lessons, when the teachers told us in edifying tones about World War I – assuming the topic fell within the curriculum and that

Verdun fell within the topic – then all eyes would turn toward
Drüng, and at such times Drüng acquired a special, fleeting
glory, for it was not often that we had history, or that World
War I fell within the curriculum, and still less often was it
permitted or appropriate to talk about Verdun . . .

The candle was hissing now, hot wax was bubbling in the
cardboard holder; then the unsupported wick toppled over into
the melted remains – but suddenly the room was filled with light
and I was ashamed of my tears, a light that was cold and naked
and gave the drab room a spurious clarity and cleanliness . . .

It was not until I felt myself grasped by the shoulders that I
realized the door had opened and two people had been sent to
carry me into the operating room. I shot another glance at
Drüng, lying there with pinched lips; then they had laid me back
on the stretcher and were carrying me out.

The doctor looked tired and irritable. He watched without
interest as the stretcher-bearers placed me on a table under a
glaring lamp; the rest of the room was shrouded in ruddy darkness. The doctor came closer, and I could see him more clearly:
his coarse skin was sallow, with purple shadows, and his thick
black hair covered his head like a cap. He read the label attached
to my chest, I noticed the cigarette smell on his breath, and I
could see the whitish rolls of fat on his neck and the mask of
weary despair over his face.

'Dina,' he called softly, 'take it off.'

He stepped back, and from the ruddy darkness emerged a
woman's figure in a white smock; her hair was all wrapped up in
a pale-green cloth, and now that she was close, leaning over me
and carefully cutting the bandage over my forehead, I saw from
the serene, pale oval of her kindly face that she must be blonde.
I was still crying, and through my tears her face appeared melting
and blurred, and her great soft light-brown eyes seemed to be
weeping too, while the doctor seemed hard and dry even through
my tears.

With a sudden movement she tore the hard, bloody rag from
my wound, I screamed and let the tears flow on. The doctor

stood scowling at the edge of the circle of light, the smoke from his cigarette reaching us in sharp blue puffs. Dina's face was quiet while she bent over me, touching my head with her fingers as she began to sponge my clotted hair.

'Shave it!' said the doctor brusquely, tossing his cigarette butt angrily onto the floor.

Now the vice of pain renewed its attacks as the Russian nurse began to shave the filthy, matted hair around the gaping wound. Once again the discs started revolving and eerily overlapping, I had moments of unconsciousness, then I would come to again, and during those waking seconds I could feel the tears flowing more and more freely, running down my cheeks and collecting between shirt and collar, compulsively, as if a well had been drilled.

'Don't cry, damn it!' shouted the doctor from time to time, and because I neither could nor would stop he shouted: 'You ought to be ashamed of yourself!' But I was not ashamed, I was aware only of Dina now and again resting her hands in a caress on my neck, and I knew it was futile to try and explain to the doctor why I had to cry. What did I know of him or he of me, of filth and lice, Drüng's face and nine school years that came punctually to an end when the war broke out?

'Damn it,' he shouted, 'for God's sake shut up!'

Then he suddenly came closer, his face looming unbelievably huge, fiercely stern, as he approached, and for one second I felt the first boring of the knife, then saw nothing more and gave only one shrill scream.

They had closed the door behind me, turned the key, and I found myself back in the first room. My candle was still flickering, sending its fleeting light over everything it encountered. I walked very slowly, I was scared, it was all so quiet, and I felt no more pain. Never before had I been so entirely without pain, so empty. I recognized my stretcher by the rumpled blankets, looked at the candle, still burning just as I had left it. The wick was floating in liquid wax, one tiny tip sticking up just enough for it to burn, and any moment now it would be submerged. I patted my pockets apprehensively, but they were empty, I ran back to the door, rattled the handle, shouted, rattled, shouted. Surely they couldn't leave us in the dark! But outside no one seemed to hear; and when I went back the candle was still burning, the wick was still floating, a tiny piece was still sticking up just enough for it to burn and produce an irregular, flickering light; this piece of wick seemed to have got smaller; in another second we would be in the dark.

'Drüng,' I called, scared, 'Drüng!'

'Yes?' came his voice. 'What's the matter?'

I felt my heart stand still, and all about me there was no sound save the appallingly quiet consuming of this candle end, on the verge of going out.

'Yes?' he asked again. 'What's the matter?'

I stepped to the left, bent down, and looked at him: he was lying there laughing. He was laughing very softly and painfully, and there was gentleness too in his smile. He had thrown back the blankets, and through a great hole in his stomach I could see the green canvas of the stretcher. He was lying there quite quietly, and seemed to be waiting. I looked at him for a long time, the laughing mouth, the hole in his stomach, the hair: it was Drüng.

'Well, what's the matter?' he asked again.

'The candle,' I whispered, looking into the light; it was still burning, I saw its radiance as, yellow and fitful, forever expiring and forever burning again, it illumined the whole room. I heard Drüng sit up, the stretcher creaked softly, the corner of a blanket was pushed aside, and now I was looking at him again.

'Don't be scared,' he shook his head and went on: 'The light won't go out, it'll burn for ever and ever, I know it will.'

But the next instant his pale face seemed to disintegrate still further; trembling, he grasped my arm, I could feel his thin, hard fingers. 'Look,' he said in a frightened whisper, 'now it's going out.'

But the anchorless wick was still floating in the cardboard holder, it was still not quite submerged.

'No,' I said, 'it should have gone out long ago, there wasn't enough to last even two minutes.'

'Oh Christ!' he shouted, his face distorted, and he slammed his hand down onto the light, jarring the stretcher so that the iron clanged, and for one second we were enveloped in greenish darkness, but when he lifted his trembling hand the wick was still floating, it was still light, and through the hole in Drüng's stomach I was looking at a pale yellow spot on the wall behind him.

'It's no use,' he said, lying back on his stretcher, 'you'd better lie down too, we'll just have to wait.'

I pushed my stretcher right up close to his so that the iron bars were touching, and as I lay down the light was between us, flickering and unsteady, always certain and always uncertain, for it ought to have gone out long ago, but it did not go out; and sometimes we raised our heads at the same time and looked at one another in fear when the convulsive flame seemed to become shorter; and before our despairing eyes was the dark oblong of the door, surrounded by a bright band of shining light . . .

. . . and so we lay there waiting, filled with fear and hope, shivering and yet warmed by the panic that seized our limbs when the flame threatened to go out and our green faces met over the cardboard holder as it stood in the midst of those moving lights that flowed around us like soundless wraiths, and suddenly we saw that the light must have gone out, for the wick was submerged, no tip stuck out over the waxen surface now, and yet it was still light – until our amazed eyes saw the figure of Dina who had come in to us through the locked door, and we knew it was all right to smile now, and we took her outstretched hands and followed her . . .

The Ration Runners

In the dark vault of the sky the stars hung like muted dots of leaden silver. Suddenly what had seemed to be random constellations began to move: the gleaming dots approached each other, grouping themselves into a pointed arch whose symmetrical curves were held together at their apex by a star that outshone all the rest. Scarcely had I taken in this minor miracle when at the lower end of each arching curve a star detached itself, and the two dots slid slowly downward to sink out of sight in the unending blackness. Fear stirred and gradually spread within me, for now, two by two, left and right, they proceeded to sink into the blackness, and from time to time I seemed to hear a hiss as their light went out. And so they all fell, one star after another, each pair gleaming softly as they sank together, until only the largest star of all remained up there, the one that had held the pointed arch together. It seemed to waver, tremble, and hesitate . . . then it sank too, slowly and solemnly, with an oppressive solemnity; and as it approached the blackness beneath, my fear swelled like some terrible travail, and at the very moment when the great star reached the bottom and, despite my fear, I waited with bated breath for total blackness to cover the vaulted sky, at that very moment the darkness exploded with an appalling detonation . . .

. . . I woke up, I could still feel the air quivering from the real blast that had woken me. Part of the earth wall in front of our foxhole now rested on my head and shoulders, and the breath of the grenade still smouldered in the black and silent air. I brushed off the dirt, and as I leaned forward to pull the ground-sheet over my head and light a cigarette, I could tell from Hans's yawn that he had been asleep too and was now awake; he held out his forearm to show me the phosphorescent dial of his watch, saying softly: 'Punctual as the Devil himself, on the dot of two, you'd better get going now.' Our heads met under the groundsheet. As I held the match over Hans's pipe I glanced at his thin face: it betrayed no emotion whatsoever.

We smoked in silence. In the dark there was no sound save the innocuous rumble of tractors bringing up ammunition. Silence and darkness seemed to have become one, lying like some enormous weight on the backs of our necks . . .

When I had finished my cigarette, Hans repeated softly: 'You'd better get going, and don't forget to take him with you, he's lying up there by the old Flak emplacement.' And when I had clambered out of my hole he added: 'There's only half of him, you know, in a groundsheet.'

I crossed the torn-up earth, groping my way with my hands, until I reached the path that over the months had been trodden by dispatch runners and ration runners. I had slung my rifle over my shoulders and tucked the old cloth bag securely into one pocket. After a couple of hundred yards I could already make out darker patches in the darkness: trees, the remains of houses, and finally what was left of the shelled hut of the old Flak emplacement. I listened nervously, hoping to hear the voices of the others, but even when I got closer and could clearly see the dark square pit where the anti-aircraft gun had stood, I still couldn't hear anything, but then I did see them, the others, squatting on old ammunition cases like great mute birds in the night, and it struck me as unspeakably depressing that they were not exchanging a single word. At their feet lay a bundle wrapped in a groundsheet, just like those bundles we used to lug off with the rest of our equipment from the uniform stores to sort the hideous camphor-reeking stuff in our dorms and try it on for size. It was strange that on this night, in the midst of the reality of war, I should recall our old barracks life more concretely and vividly than ever before, and I shuddered to think that the fellow lying there in the groundsheet, a formless mass, had once been yelled at like the rest of us when he was issued the same kind of bundle from the uniform stores. 'Evening,' I said in a whisper, and I got an indistinct murmur in reply.

I squatted down beside the others on the nearest pile of 20-millimetre cardboard shell cases: they had been lying around here for months, some of them still full, just as they had been abandoned by the Flak in its confused and hurried flight.

No one moved. We all sat there, our hands in our pockets, waiting and brooding, and each one of us must have glanced from time to time at the mute, dark bundle at our feet. At last the platoon dispatch runner got up, saying:

'Shall we go?'

Instead of replying we all rose; it was so futile to go on squatting there, it didn't make things any better for us. What difference did it make, after all, whether we squatted here or up front in our holes, and besides, we had heard there was a chocolate issue today, maybe even some schnapps, reason enough to get to the chow line as fast as possible.

'First group, how many?'

'Five,' answered a subdued voice.

'Second?'

'Six.'

'And third?'

'Four,' I answered.

'There are two of us,' counted the dispatch runner in an undertone, 'O.K., let's call it twenty-one, shall we? I hear it's hash.'

'O.K.'

The dispatch runner was the first to go over to the bundle; we watched him bend down, then he said: 'We'll each take one corner, it's a young sapper, half a sapper.'

We bent down too, and each of us grasped a corner of the groundsheet; then the dispatch runner said: 'Let's go,' and we lifted the bundle and trudged off, towards the outskirts of the village . . .

Every dead man is as heavy as the whole earth, but this half-a-dead-man was as heavy as the world. It was as if he had absorbed the sum of all the pain and all the burdens of the entire universe. We panted and groaned and, by tacit consent, set down our load after a couple of dozen yards.

And the distances became shorter and shorter, the half-a-sapper became heavier and heavier, as if he were absorbing more and more burdens. It seemed as if the earth's weak crust must collapse beneath this weight, and when in our exhaustion we lowered our bundle to the ground I felt as if we would never manage to lift the dead man up again. At the same time I had the feeling the bundle was growing beyond all measurable limits. The three at the other corners seemed infinitely far away, so far that if I called they couldn't possibly hear me. And I was growing too, my hands became enormous, my head assumed nightmarish proportions, but the dead man, the corpse-bundle, was puffing up like some monstrous tube, as if it would never stop drinking in the blood of all battlefields of all wars.

All the laws of gravity and dimension were suspended and extended into infinity, so-called reality was inflated by the dim and shadowy laws of another reality, one which made a mockery of them.

The half-a-sapper swelled and swelled like a monstrous sponge saturating itself with leaden blood. Cold sweat broke out over my body, mingling with that foul dirt that had accumulated over it during the long weeks. I could smell myself, and I smelled like a corpse . . .

As I trudged on and on, carrying the sapper, obeying that strange urge that compelled us each to take hold of one corner again at a certain instant; as we went on and on, always a dozen yards or so at a time, lugging the burden of the world towards the outskirts of the village, I almost lost consciousness under the impact of an appalling fear that flowed from that steadily growing bundle and filled my veins like poison. I saw no more, I heard nothing, and yet I was aware of every detail of what happened . . .

I had not heard the grenade being fired or the whine of its approach; the explosion ripped apart the whole fine mesh of dreamlike, semiconscious agony; with empty hands I stared into space, while far away, somewhere along a slope, the echo of the explosion reverberated like peals of laughter; in front, behind, on both sides, I could hear that strange, laughing echo, as if I were caught in a valley between high mountains, and the sound reached my ears like the tinny jangle of those patriotic songs that used to crawl up and down the barracks walls. With an almost disembodied curiosity I waited expectantly for pain to make itself felt somewhere on my body or for the sensation of warm, flowing blood. Nothing, nothing at all. But suddenly I realized that my feet were standing half over an empty space, that the front half of each foot was teetering over a void, and when I looked down, with the casual curiosity of someone just waking up, I saw, blacker than the surrounding blackness, a great crater at my feet . . .

I stepped gamely forward into the crater, but I did not fall, I did not sink; on and on I walked, always on marvellously soft ground beneath the absolute darkness of the vaulted sky. I kept wondering, as I walked along, whether I should report twenty-one, seventeen, or fourteen to the quartermaster-sergeant . . . until the great, yellow, shining star rose before me and planted itself firmly in the vault of the sky; then the other stars, softly gleaming, found their places, two by two, forming a closed triangle. I knew then that I had reached a different destination and that what I really had to report was four and a half, and as I smiled and said over to myself: four and a half, a great kindly voice spoke: Five!

Reunion in the Avenue

Sometimes, when it got really quiet, when the hoarse growl of the machine guns had died down and that hideous harsh sound of grenade launchers had ceased, when over the lines there hovered an indefinable something that our fathers might have called peace: during those hours we would interrupt our lice-picking or our shallow sleep, and Lieutenant Hecker's long hands would finger the catch on the ammunition case that was let into the wall of our dugout and known to us as our bar. He would tug at the leather strap, making the prong of the clasp snap out of its hole and disclose our property in all its glory: on the left the Lieutenant's bottle, on the right mine, and in the middle, jointly owned, our most treasured possession, saved up for the hours when it got really quiet . . .

Between the grey-white bottles of potato schnapps stood two bottles of genuine French cognac, the finest we had ever tasted. In some manner that defied explanation, passing through untold opportunities for pilfering and the very heart of the jungle of corruption, genuine Hennessy would turn up at intervals in our front-line dugouts where we were fighting dirt, lice, and despair. The youngsters, with the craving of pallid children for sweet things, shuddered at the mere mention of schnapps, so we gave them chocolate and candy in exchange for their share of this golden elixir, and seldom, I imagine, was any barter concluded with greater satisfaction to both parties.

'Come on,' Hecker used to say, after buttoning on a clean collar – if one was available – and running his hand voluptuously over his freshly shaved chin. I would slowly get to my feet and emerge from the shadowy depths of our dugout, lethargically

brush the wisps of straw from my uniform, and confine myself
to the only ritual for which I could still summon enough energy:
comb my hair, and slowly, with a dedication bordering on the
unnatural, wash my hands in Hecker's shaving water – some
coffee dregs in a tin can. Meanwhile Hecker, patiently waiting
for me to clean my nails, would first set up an ammunition case
between us as a kind of table, then take out his handkerchief and
wipe our two schnapps glasses: thick, solid affairs that we guarded
as carefully as our tobacco. By the time he had dug the big
package of cigarettes out from the inner recesses of his pocket,
I had completed my preparations.

It was usually in the afternoon, we had pushed aside the
blanket hanging in front of our dugout, and sometimes a bit of
modest sunshine warmed our feet . . .

Our eyes met, we touched glasses, drank, and smoked. Our
silence had a quality of solemn rapture. The only evidence of the
enemy was the sound of a sniper's bullet striking the ground,
with scrupulous punctuality and at regular intervals, just in front
of the beams shoring up the earth bank at the entrance to our
dugout. With a small, rather endearing 'flup' the bullet would
whir into the crumbling earth. It often reminded me of the
modest, barely audible scurrying of a field mouse across a path
on a quiet afternoon. There was something soothing about this
sound, for it reassured us that this delectable hour now about to
begin was not a dream, not an illusion, but part of our real life.

Only after the fourth or fifth glass would we start to talk.
Beneath the exhausted rubble of our hearts, this miraculous
potion awakened something strangely precious that our fathers
might have called nostalgia.

About the war, the present, we had said all we had to say. Too
often and too intimately had we seen the bared teeth in its
hideous face, too often had its nauseating breath set our hearts
quivering as we listened on dark nights to the wounded pleading
in two languages between the lines. We loathed it too deeply to
be able to believe in the cant sent up like soap bubbles by the
riffraff on both sides to invest it with the virtues of a 'mission'.

Nor could the future serve as a topic. The future was a black tunnel full of sharp corners that we were going to bump into, and we lived in dread of it, for the appalling existence we led as soldiers who had to wish for the war to be lost had hollowed out our hearts.

We talked about the past; about those meagre rudiments of what our fathers might have called life. About that all too brief span of human memories caught between the rotting corpse of the Weimar Republic and that bloated monster of a state whose pay we had to pocket.

'Picture a little café,' said Hecker, 'under some trees, maybe, in the fall. The smell of moisture and decaying leaves in the air, and you're translating a poem by Verlaine. You're wearing very light shoes, and later, when dusk falls in opaque clouds, you scuff your way home – know what I mean? You scuff your feet through the wet leaves and look into the faces of the girls coming towards you . . .' He filled our glasses, his hands as quiet as those of a kindly doctor operating on a child, we touched glasses and drank . . . 'Maybe one of the girls smiles at you, you smile back, and you both go on your way without turning round. That little smile you exchanged will never die, never, I tell you . . . It may be your signal of recognition when you meet again in another life . . . an absurd little smile . . .'

A marvellously youthful light came into his eyes, he looked at me and laughed, and I smiled too, grasped the bottle and poured. We drank three or four glasses, one after another, and no tobacco ever tasted finer than the one that blended with the exquisite aroma of the cognac.

At intervals the sniper's bullet would remind us that time was dripping remorselessly away; and behind our pleasure and our enjoyment of the hour there was again that inexorable threat to our existence that could wipe us out with a bursting shell, a sentry's warning cry, or a command to attack or retreat. We began to drink faster, our conversation grew more distraught, the gentle contentment in our eyes was joined by passion and hatred; and when, as was inevitable, the bottom of the bottle became visible, Hecker would become unutterably sad, his eyes would turn towards me like blurred discs, and in a low, almost incoherent voice he would begin whispering: 'That girl, you know, lived at the end of an avenue, and the last time I was on leave . . .'

That was the signal for me to cut him short. 'Lieutenant,' I would say, coldly and severely, 'be quiet, d'you hear?' He had told me himself: 'When I start talking about a girl who lived at the end of an avenue, it's time for you to tell me to shut up, d'you understand? You must, you must!'

And I obeyed this command, although it went against the grain, for when I reminded him Hecker would stop in his tracks, the light in his eyes would go out, they would become hard and sober, and around his mouth the old creases of bitterness would reappear . . .

On that particular day, however, the one I am talking about, everything was unusual. We had been issued underwear, brand-new underwear, and a fresh supply of cognac. I had shaved and even gone so far as to wash my feet in the tin can: in fact, I practically took a bath, for they had even sent us new socks, socks with white borders that were still really white . . .

Hecker was leaning back on our pallet, smoking and watching me wash. It was absolutely silent outside, but this silence was evil and numbing, a threatening silence, and I could tell from Hecker's hands when he lighted a fresh cigarette from the old one that he was on edge and afraid: we were all afraid, everyone who was still human was afraid.

Suddenly we heard the faint scurrying sound the sniper's bullet always made in the earth bank, and with this gentle sound the silence ceased to be unnerving. With one breath we both laughed out loud; Hecker jumped to his feet, stamped around a bit, and shouted like a child: 'Hooray, hooray, now let's get drunk, drunk in honour of our friend who always fires at the same place and always at the wrong place!'

He unfastened the catch, slapped me on the shoulder, and waited patiently until I had pulled my boots on again and seated myself in readiness for our drinking session. Hecker spread a clean handkerchief over the case and drew two light-brown cigars of impressive length from his breast pocket.

'You can't beat that,' he laughed, 'cognac and a good cigar!' We touched glasses, drank, and smoked with slow, rapturous enjoyment.

'How about you talking for a change?' cried Hecker. 'Come on, tell me something about yourself,' he said, giving me a serious look. 'You know something? You've never told me a thing, you've always let me rattle on.'

'There's not much to tell,' I observed in a low voice, and then I looked at him, poured some more cognac, waited, and then we drank together, and it was marvellous to feel the cool, superbly warming drink flowing into us in a stream of dark gold. 'You see,' I began diffidently, 'I'm younger than you and a bit older. I was hopeless in school so I had to quit and learn a trade, they apprenticed me to a cabinetmaker. That was pretty hard to take at first, but in time, after a year or so, I began to enjoy the work. There's something tremendously satisfying about working with wood. You make yourself a drawing on some nice white paper, get your wood ready, clean, fine-grained planks, and then you plane them with loving care while the smell of wood rises into your nostrils. I believe I would have made quite a good cabinetmaker, but at nineteen I was called up, and I've never recovered from the first shock I got after passing through the barracks gates, not even now, after six years, that's why I don't talk much . . . with you fellows it's a bit different . . .' I blushed, it was the longest speech I had ever made in my life.

Hecker looked at me reflectively. 'I see,' he said. 'I like the sound of that: cabinetmaker.'

'But haven't you ever had a girl?' he suddenly resumed, raising his voice, and I knew at once that I would soon have to cut him short again. 'Never ever? Haven't you ever leaned your head on a soft shoulder and smelled her hair . . . never?' This time it was he who refilled our glasses, and with these two drinks the bottle was empty. Hecker glanced round with a look of terrible sadness. 'No walls here to smash a bottle against, eh? Wait a minute,' he shouted suddenly with a wild laugh, 'our friend must have something too, let's have him smash it.'

He stepped forward and placed the bottle on the spot where the sniper's bullets always struck the earth, and before I could stop him he had taken the next bottle out of our bar, opened it, and filled our glasses. We touched glasses, and at the same moment a gentle 'ping' sounded from outside on the bank: we looked up in alarm and saw how for an instant the bottle stood steady, almost rigid, but the next instant its top half slid off, leaving the bottom half still standing. The chunk of broken glass rolled into the ditch almost to our feet, and all I remember is being frightened, frightened from the moment the bottle was shattered . . .

At the same time I was seized by a profound indifference while I helped Hecker empty the second bottle as fast as he filled our glasses. Yes, fear and at the same time indifference. Hecker was frightened too, I could tell; our agonized eyes avoided each other, and that day I couldn't summon the strength to interrupt him when he started talking about the girl . . .

'You know,' he said urgently, looking beyond me, 'she lived at the end of an avenue, and the last time I was on leave it was in the fall, real fall weather, late afternoon, and I can't begin to describe how beautiful the avenue was –.' A wild, rapturous, yet somehow frenzied happiness leaped into his eyes, and if only for the sake of that happiness I was glad I had not interrupted him; as he went on talking he worked his hands like a person trying to give shape to something without knowing how, and I could feel him searching for the right expressions to describe the avenue to me. I filled our glasses, we drank up, I filled them again, we tossed them back . . .

'The avenue,' he said huskily, almost stammering, 'the avenue was all golden – I'm not kidding, it really was, black trees with gold, and a greyish blue shimmer in the gold – I was in ecstasy as I walked slowly along under the trees as far as that house, I felt as if that fantastic beauty had spun a web around me, and I drank in the intoxicating transience of our human happiness.

Do you know what I mean? That magical certainty moved me inexpressibly . . . and . . . and . . .'

Hecker was silent for a while, evidently searching for words again; I poured out some more cognac, we touched glasses, and drank: at that precise instant the bottom half of the bottle on the bank was shattered too, and with maddening deliberation the pieces of glass rolled one after another into the ditch.

I was startled to see Hecker jump to his feet, lean down, and thrust the blanket aside. I held onto his sleeve, and I knew now why I had been frightened all along. 'Let go!' he shouted. 'Let go . . . I'm going – I'm going to the avenue . . .' Outside I stood next to him, holding the bottle. 'I'm going,' whispered Hecker, 'I'm going all the way along it, right to the end where the house is! There's a brown iron gate in front of it, and she lives upstairs, and . . .' I ducked hurriedly as a bullet whistled past me into the bank, landing just where the bottle had stood.

Hecker was whispering incoherent, rambling words, on his face a look of serene happiness, mild and gentle now, and there might still have been time to call him back as he had ordered me to. From his ramblings I could distinguish only the same words, repeated over and over: 'I'm going – don't try to stop me, I'm going to the house where my girl lives . . .'

I felt a real coward, crouching there in the ground holding the bottle of cognac, and guilty at being sober, cruelly sober, while Hecker wore an expression of unutterably sweet, serene drunkenness. He was staring straight ahead at the enemy lines between black sunflower stalks and shelled farmhouses; I watched him narrowly, he smoked a cigarette.

'Lieutenant,' I called softly, holding out the bottle, 'come and have a drink,' and when I tried to stand up I realized I was drunk too, and I cursed myself to the very depths of my being for not having called him back soon enough, for now it was obviously too late. He hadn't heard me call, and just as I was about to open my mouth to call him again, at least to entice him back out of danger with the bottle, I heard the clear, high-pitched 'ping' of an exploding bullet. With appalling suddenness Hecker turned round, gave me one brief and blissful smile, placed his cigarette on the bank, and collapsed, falling slowly, slowly backward. An icy hand gripped my heart, the bottle slid from my grasp, and I watched in shock and dismay as the cognac, gently gurgling, flowed out and formed a little puddle. Once again it was very quiet, and the silence was menacing . . .

At last I found the courage to raise my eyes and look into Hecker's face: his cheeks had caved in, his eyes were black and rigid, yet his face still bore a hint of that smile which had blossomed there as he whispered those frenzied words. I knew he was dead. But all of a sudden I started shouting, shouting like a madman. I leaned over the bank, oblivious to all caution, and shouted to the next dugout: 'Heini! Help! Heini, Hecker's dead!' and without waiting for an answer I sank sobbing to the ground, seized by unspeakable horror, for Hecker's head had raised itself a little, barely perceptibly, but visibly, and blood was welling out of it and a ghastly yellowish-white substance that could only be his brains; it flowed on and on, and frozen with terror I could only think: Where can all this blood be coming from, just from his head? The whole floor of our dugout was covered with blood, the clayey soil didn't absorb it, and the blood reached the spot where I knelt beside the empty bottle . . .

I was alone in the world with Hecker's blood, for Heini didn't answer and the gentle swish of the sniper's bullet was no longer audible . . .

Suddenly, however, the silence was rent by an explosion, I scrambled to my feet, and at the same moment something struck me in the back, although strangely enough I felt no pain. I sank forward with my head on Hecker s chest, and while noise sprang to life around me, the frantic barking of the machine gun from Heini's dugout and the sickening impact of the grenade launchers that we called pipe organs, I became quite calm: for mingling with Hecker's dark blood that still covered the bottom of the dugout was a lighter, miraculously light blood that I knew was warm and my own; and I sank down and down until I found myself, smiling happily, at the entrance to that avenue which

Hecker hadn't known how to describe, because the trees were bare, solitude and desolation were nesting among wan shadows, and hope died in my heart, while far off, at an immense distance, I could see Hecker's beckoning figure outlined against a soft golden light . . .

In the Darkness

'Light the candle,' said a voice.

There was no sound, only that exasperating, aimless rustle of someone trying to get to sleep.

'Light the candle, I say,' came the voice again, on a sharper note this time.

The sounds at last became distinguishable as someone moving, throwing aside the blanket, and sitting up; this was apparent from the breathing, which now came from above. The straw rustled too.

'Well?' said the voice.

'The lieutenant said we weren't to light the candle except on orders, in an emergency . . .' said a younger, diffident voice.

'Light the candle, I say, you little pip-squeak,' the older voice shouted back.

He sat up now too, their heads were on the same level in the dark, their breathing was parallel.

The one who had first spoken irritably followed the movements of the other, who had tucked the candle away somewhere in his pack. His breathing relaxed when he eventually heard the sound of the matchbox.

The match flared up, and there was light: a sparse yellow light.

Their eyes met. Invariably, as soon as there was enough light, their eyes met. Yet they knew one another so well, much too well. They almost hated each other, so familiar was each to each; they knew one another's very smell, the smell of every pore, so to speak, but still their eyes met, those of the older man and the younger. The younger one was pale and slight with a nondescript face, and the older one was pale and slight and unshaven with a nondescript face.

'Now listen,' said the older man, calmer now, 'when are you ever going to learn that you don't do everything the lieutenants tell you?'

'He'll . . .' the younger one tried to begin.

'He won't do a thing,' said the older one, in a sharper tone again and lighting a cigarette from the candle. 'He'll keep his trap shut, and if he doesn't, and I don't happen to be around, then tell him to wait till I get back, it was me who lit the candle, understand? Do you understand?'

'Yessir.'

'To hell with that Yessir crap, just Yes when you're talking to me. And undo your belt,' he was shouting again now, 'take that damn crappy belt off when you go to sleep.'

The younger man looked at him nervously and took off his belt, placing it beside him in the straw.

'Roll your coat up into a pillow. That's right. O.K. . . . and now go to sleep, I'll wake you when it's time for you to die . . .'

The younger man rolled onto his side and tried to sleep. All that was visible was the young brown hair, matted and untidy, a very thin neck, and the empty shoulders of his uniform tunic. The candle flickered gently, letting its meagre light swing back and forth in the dark dugout like a great yellow butterfly uncertain where to settle.

The older man stayed as he was, knees drawn up, puffing out cigarette smoke at the ground in front of him. The ground was dark brown, here and there white blade marks showed where the spade had cut through a root or, a little closer to the surface, a tuber. The roof consisted of a few planks with a ground sheet thrown over them, and in the spaces between the planks the groundsheet sagged a little because the earth lying on top of it was heavy, heavy and wet. Outside it was raining. The soft swish of steadily falling water sounded indescribably persistent, and the older man, still staring fixedly at the ground, now noticed a thin trickle of water oozing into the dugout under the roof. The tiny stream backed up slightly on encountering some loose earth, then flowed on past the obstacle until it reached the next one, which was the man's feet, and the ever-growing tide flowed all around the man's feet until his black boots lay in the water just like a peninsula. The man spat his cigarette butt into the puddle and lit another from the candle. In doing so he took the candle down from the edge of the dugout and placed it beside him on an ammunition case. The half where the younger man was lying was almost in darkness, reached now by the swaying light in brief spasms only, and these gradually subsided.

'Go to sleep, damn you,' said the older man. 'D'you hear? Go to sleep!'

'Yessir . . . yes,' came the faint voice, obviously wider awake than before, when it had been dark.

'Hold on,' said the older man, less harshly again. 'A couple more cigarettes and then I'll put it out, and at least we'll drown in the dark.'

He went on smoking, sometimes turning his head to the left, where the boy was lying, but he spat the second butt into the steadily growing puddle, lit the third, and still he could tell from the breathing beside him that the kid couldn't sleep.

He then took the spade, thrust it into the soft earth, and made a little mud wall behind the blanket forming the entrance. Behind this wall he heaped up a second layer of earth. With a spadeful of earth he covered the puddle at his feet. Outside there was no sound save the gentle swish of the rain; little by little, the earth lying on top of the groundsheet had evidently become saturated, for water was now beginning to drip from above too.

'Oh shit,' muttered the older man. 'Are you asleep?'

'No.'

The man spat the third cigarette butt over the mud wall and blew out the candle. He pulled up his blanket again, worked his feet into a comfortable position, and lay back with a sigh. It was quite silent and quite dark, and again the only sound was that aimless rustle of someone trying to get to sleep, and the swish of the rain, very gentle.

'Willi's been wounded,' the boy's voice said suddenly, after a few minutes' silence. The voice was more awake than ever, in fact not even sleepy.

'What d'you mean?' asked the man in reply.

'Just that – wounded,' came the younger voice, with something like triumph in it, pleased that it knew some important piece of news which the older voice obviously knew nothing about. 'Wounded while he was shitting.'

'You're nuts,' said the man; then he gave another sigh and went on: 'That's what I call a real break, I never heard such luck. One day you come back from leave and the next day you get wounded while you're shitting. Is it serious?'

'No,' said the boy with a laugh, 'though actually it's not minor either. A bullet fracture, but in the arm.'

'A bullet fracture in the arm! You come back from leave and while you're shitting you get wounded, a bullet fracture in the arm! What a break . . . How did it happen?'

'When they went for water last evening,' came the younger voice, quite animated now. 'When they went for water, they were going down the hill at the back, carrying their water cans, and Willi told Sergeant Schubert: "I've got to shit, Sergeant!" "Nothing doing," said the sergeant. But Willi couldn't hold on any longer so he just ran off, pulled down his pants, and bang! A grenade. And they had to actually pull up his pants for him. His left arm was wounded, and his right arm was holding it, so he ran off like that to get it bandaged, with his pants around his ankles. They all laughed, everyone laughed, even Sergeant Schubert laughed.' He added the last few words almost apologetically, as if to excuse his own laughter, because he was laughing now . . .

But the older man wasn't laughing.

'Light!' he said with an oath. 'Here, give me the matches, let's have some light!' He struck a match, cursing as it flared up. 'At

least I want some light, even if I don't get wounded. At least let's
have some light, the least they can do is give us enough candles
if they want to play war. Light! Light!' He was shouting again
as he lit another cigarette.

The younger voice had sat up again and was poking around
with a spoon in a greasy can held on his knees.

And there they sat, crouching side by side, without a word, in
the yellow light.

The man smoked aggressively, and the boy was already looking somewhat greasy: his childish face smeared, bread crumbs
sticking to his matted hair around most of his hairline.

The boy then proceeded to scrape out the grease can with a
piece of bread.

All of a sudden there was silence: the rain had stopped.
Neither of them moved, they looked at each other, the man with
the cigarette in his hand, the boy holding the bread in his
trembling fingers. It was uncannily quiet, they took a few breaths,
and then heard rain still dripping somewhere from the groundsheet.

'Hell,' said the older man, 'D'you suppose the sentry's still
there? I can't hear a thing.'

The boy put the bread into his mouth and threw the can into
the straw beside him.

'I don't know,' said the boy, 'they're going to let us know
when it's our turn to relieve.'

The older man got up quickly. He blew out the light, jammed
on his steel helmet, and thrust aside the blanket. What came
through the opening was not light. Just cool damp darkness.
The man snipped out his cigarette and stuck his head outside.

'Hell,' he muttered outside, 'not a thing. Hey!' he called
softly. Then his dark head reappeared inside, and he asked:
'Where's the next dugout?'

The boy groped his way to his feet and stood next to the other
man in the opening.

'Quiet!' said the man suddenly, in a sharp, low tone. 'Something's crawling around out there.'

They peered ahead. It was true, in the silent darkness there was a sound of someone crawling, and all of a sudden an unearthly snapping sound that made them both jump. It sounded as if someone had flung a live cat against the wall: the sound of breaking bones.

'Hell,' muttered the older man, 'there's something funny going on. Where's the sentry?' 'Over there,' said the boy, groping in the dark for the other man's hand and lifting it towards the right.

'Over there,' he repeated, 'that's where the dugout is too.'

'Wait here,' said the older man, 'and better get your rifle, just in case.'

Once again they heard that sickening snapping sound, then silence, and someone crawling.

The older man crept forward through the mud, occasionally halting and quietly listening, until after a few yards he finally heard a muffled voice; then he saw a faint gleam of light from the ground, felt around till he found the entrance, and called 'Hey, chum!'

The voice stopped, the light went out, a blanket was pushed aside, and a man's dark head came up out of the ground.

'What's up?'

'Where's the sentry?'

'Over there – right here.'

'Where?'

'Hey there, Neuer! . . . Hey there!'

No answer: the crawling sound had stopped, all sound had stopped, there was only darkness out there, silent darkness. 'God damn it, that's queer,' said the voice of the man who had come up out of the ground. 'Hey there! . . . That's funny, he was standing right here by the dugout, only a few feet away.' He pulled himself up over the edge and stood beside the man who had called him.

'There was someone crawling around out there,' said the man who had come across from the other dugout. 'I know there was. The bastard's quiet now.'

'Better have a look,' said the man who had come up out of the ground. 'Shall we take a look?'

'Hm, there certainly ought to be a sentry here.'

'You fellows are next.'

'I know, but . . .'

'Ssh!'

Once again they could hear someone crawling out there, perhaps twenty feet away.

'God damn it,' said the man who had come up out of the ground, 'you're right.'

'Maybe someone still alive from last night, trying to crawl away.'

'Or new ones.'

'But what about the sentry, for God's sake?'

'Shall we go?'

'Okay.'

Both men instantly dropped to the ground and started to move forward, crawling through the mud. From down there, from a worm's-eye view, everything looked different. Every minutest elevation in the soil became a mountain range behind which, far off, something strange was visible: a slightly lighter darkness, the sky. Pistol in hand, they crawled on, yard by yard through the mud.

'God damn it,' whispered the man who had come up out of the ground, 'a Russki from last night.'

His companion also soon bumped into a corpse, a mute, leaden bundle. Suddenly they were silent, holding their breath: there was that cracking sound again, quite close, as if someone had been given a terrific wallop on the jaw. Then they heard someone panting.

'Hey,' called the man who had come up out of the ground, 'who's there?'

The call silenced all sound, the very air seemed to hold its breath, until a quavering voice spoke: 'It's me . . .' 'God damn it, what the hell are you doing out there, you old arsehole, driving us all nuts?' shouted the man who had come up out of the ground. 'I'm looking for something,' came the voice again.

The two men had got to their feet and now walked over to the spot where the voice was coming from the ground.

'I'm looking for a pair of shoes,' said the voice, but now they were standing next to him. Their eyes had become accustomed to the dark, and the could see corpses lying all around, ten or a dozen, lying there like logs, black and motionless, and the sentry was squatting beside one of these logs, fumbling around its feet.

'Your job's to stick to your post,' said the man who had come up out of the ground.

The other man, the one who had summoned him out of the ground, dropped like a stone and bent over the dead man's face. The man who had been squatting suddenly covered his face with his hands and began whimpering like a cowed animal.

'Oh no,' said the man who had summoned the other out of the ground, adding in an undertone: 'I guess you need teeth too, eh? Gold teeth, eh?'

'What's that?' asked the man who had come up out of the ground, while at his feet the cringing figure whimpered louder than ever.

'Oh no,' said the first man again, and the weight of the world seemed to be lying on his breast.

'Teeth?' asked the man who had come up out of the ground, whereupon he threw himself down beside the cringing figure and ripped a cloth bag from his hand.

'Oh no!' the cringing figure cried too, and every extremity of human terror was expressed in this cry.

The man who had summoned the other out of the ground turned away, for the man who had come up out of the ground had placed his pistol against the cringing figure's head, and he pressed the trigger.

'Teeth,' he muttered, as the sound of the shot died away. 'Gold teeth.'

They walked slowly back, stepping very carefully as long as they were in the area where the dead lay.

'You fellows are on now,' said the man who had come up out of the ground, before vanishing into the ground again.

'Right,' was all the other man said, and he too crawled slowly back through the mud before vanishing into the ground again.

He could tell at once that the boy was still awake; there was that aimless rustle of someone trying to get to sleep.

'Light the candle,' he said quietly.

The yellow flame leaped up again, feebly illuminating the little hole.

'What happened?' asked the boy in alarm, catching sight of the older man's face.

'The sentry's gone, you'll have to replace him.'

'Yes,' said the youngster, 'give me the watch, will you, so I can wake the others.'

'Here.'

The older man squatted down on his straw and lit a cigarette, watching thoughtfully as the boy buckled on his belt, pulled on his coat, defused a hand grenade, and then wearily checked his machine pistol for ammunition.

'Right,' said the boy finally, 'so long now.'

'So long,' said the man, and he blew out the candle and lay in total darkness all alone in the ground . . .

Broommakers

Our maths teacher was as good-natured as he was hot-tempered. He used to come charging into the classroom – hands in pockets – spew his cigarette butt into the cuspidor to the left of the waste-paper basket, take the dais by storm and, standing by his desk, call out my name as he asked some question or other to which I never knew the answer, no matter what it was . . .

After I had floundered my way to a halt, he would walk over to me, very slowly, accompanied by the tittering of the whole class, and cuff me over the head – my long-suffering head – in his rough good-natured way, muttering: 'You boneheaded broommaker, you . . .'

It became a kind of ritual, the thought of which made me tremble throughout my school days, the more so since my knowledge of science, far from growing with increased demands, seemed to diminish. But, having duly cuffed me, he would leave me in peace, leave me to my meandering daydreams, for to try and teach me maths was a completely hopeless proposition. I dragged my 'F' after me all through those years like the heavy ball chained to a convict's feet.

What impressed me about him was that he never had a book or notes with him, not even a slip of paper: he performed his occult arts with casual ease, tossing stupendous formulas onto the blackboard with something of a tightrope walker's absolute mastery. The one thing he could not draw was circles. He was too impatient. He would wind a string around a long piece of chalk, pick the imaginary centre, and swing the chalk round with such gusto that it would snap and, with a whining screech, go bounding across the blackboard – dash – dot, dot – dash. He never managed to make the beginning and end meet, and the result was an unsightly gaping outline, truly an unacknowledged symbol of Creation rent asunder. And that sound of the squeaking, screeching, chattering chalk piled further agony on my already tortured brain: I would stir from my daydreams, look up, and the minute he caught sight of me he would rush over, pull me up by the ears, and order me to draw his circles for him. For this was an art, springing from some slumbering, innate law within me, that I mastered to near-perfection. What an exquisite feeling it was, to play with the chalk for half a second. It was a minor ecstasy, the world around me would drop away, and I was filled with a profound happiness that made up for all the agony . . . but even from this sweet oblivion I would be roused by a rough, although this time respectful, tug at my hair, and with the laughter of the entire class in my ears I would slink back to my seat like a whipped dog, incapable now of re-entering my dream-world, to wait in perpetual agony for the bell to ring . . .

It was a long time since those early days, a long time since my dreams had become more disturbing, a long time since he had dropped the '*Du*' when calling me 'a boneheaded broommaker', and there were long months of torment during which there were no circles to be drawn and I was condemned to hopeless attempts to clamber over the brittle girders of algebraical bridges, still dragging my 'F' behind me, the familiar ritual still being performed. But then when we had to volunteer for officer-training a brief test was improvised, simple but nonetheless a test, and my expression of utter wretchedness as I faced the stern examining board may have softened the maths teacher's heart, for he was so skilful in putting words into my mouth that I actually passed. Later on, however, as we shook hands with the teachers on leaving, he advised me to forgo the use of my mathematical knowledge and to be sure and avoid joining a technical unit. 'Infantry,' he whispered, 'join the infantry, that's the place for all – broommakers,' and for the last time, with a gesture that concealed his affection, he made as if to cuff me over the head – my now well-seasoned head . . .

*

Scarcely two months later, at the Odessa airfield, I was sitting crouched over my pack, in deep mud, watching a real broom-maker, the first I had ever seen.

Winter had come early, and over the nearby city the sky hung grey and comfortless between the horizons. Dingy tall buildings were visible among outlying gardens and black fences. In the distance, where the Black Sea must be, the sky was even darker, almost blue-black, as if twilight and evening came from the east. Somewhere in the background the trundling monsters were being refuelled alongside cavernous hangars, after which they trundled back and, standing there in horrible complacency, were loaded up with men, grey, tired, despairing soldiers whose eyes were devoid of all emotion but fear – for the Crimea had long since been encircled . . .

Our platoon must have been one of the last; no one spoke, and in spite of our long greatcoats we were shivering. Some of the men were eating in desperation, others were smoking, and because this was prohibited they covered their pipes with their palms and blew the smoke out in slow thin puffs.

I had plenty of time to watch the broommaker as he sat a little way off beside a garden fence. He was wearing one of those rakish-looking Russian hats, and in his bearded face the short stocky brown pipe was as broad and long as his nose. But there were peace and simplicity in his quietly working hands as they picked up the bunches of furze twigs, cut them, tied them with wire, and fastened the finished bundles in the holes of the broom handle.

I had turned round onto my stomach, lying almost flat on my pack, and all I saw was the looming silhouette of this quiet, humble man, working steadily and unhurriedly away at his brooms. Never in my life have I envied anyone as much as that broommaker, neither the top student, nor Schimski the maths brain, nor the best football player on the school team, nor even Hegenbach, whose brother had the Knight's Cross; not one of those I had ever envied as I envied that broommaker, sitting by a fence on the outskirts of Odessa and serenely smoking his pipe.

I longed secretly to catch the man's eye, for I fancied it would be comforting to look directly into that face, but I was suddenly jerked up by my coat, shouted at, and jammed into the droning aircraft, and once we had taken off and were flying high above the distracting jumble of gardens and roads and churches it would have been impossible to try and make out the broommaker.

First I squatted on my pack, but then I slipped down behind it onto the floor and, stupefied by the oppressive silence of my fellow victims, was listening to the unearthly drone of the aircraft, while the constant vibration began to make my head quiver as it leaned against the metal wall. The darkness of the narrow fuselage was relieved only by a somewhat lighter darkness up front, where the pilot sat, and this pale reflection threw an eerie light on the mute, dim figures squatting left and right and all around me on their packs.

But suddenly a strange noise tore across the sky, so real and familiar that I sat bolt upright: it was as if the hand of a giant maths teacher were drawing a massive hunk of chalk in an arc across the limitless expanse of dark sky, and the noise exactly matched the familiar one I had heard two months before: the same leap and chatter of protesting chalk.

Arc after arc was drawn across the sky by the hand of the colossus, but now, instead of being only white and dark grey, it was red on blue and purple on black, and the flashing streaks faded without completing their circles, chattered, screeched, and died away.

I suffered not for the terrified, frenzied groans of my fellow victims, or the shouting of the lieutenant vainly ordering the men to be quiet and stay where they were, or even the agonized face of the pilot. I suffered merely for those eternally uncompleted circles that flared up over the sky, in a fury of haste and hate, and never ever returned to their starting point, those botched circles whose ends never met to achieve the perfect beauty of the circle. They tormented me along with the chattering, screeching, leaping wrath of the giant hand, the hand I dreaded would grab me by the hair and cuff me brutally over the head.

Then came the real shock: I suddenly realized that this sky-splitting fury was in fact a noise: close to my head I heard a strange hiss as of a baleful, swiftly descending hand, felt a moist, hot pain, jumped up with a cry and reached out towards the sky where just then another searing yellow flash blazed up; with my right hand I held on tight to this flailing yellow snake, letting it spin its angry circle, confident that I would be able to complete the circle, for this was the one and only art I had been born to master. So I held it, guided it, the flailing, raging, jerking, chattering snake, held on to it while my breath came hot and my twitching mouth hurt and the moist pain in my head seemed to increase, and as I brought the points together, drawing the glorious round arc of the circle and gazing at it with pride, the spaces between the dots and dashes closed and an immense, hissing short circuit filled the entire circle with light and fire until the whole sky was burning, and the abrupt momentum of the plunging aircraft rent the world in two. All I could see were light and fire, and the mutilated tail of the machine, a jagged tail like the black stump of a broom fit to carry a witch riding off to her sabbath . . .

My Expensive Leg

They're giving me a chance now. They sent me a postcard telling me to come down to the Department, and I went. They were very nice to me at the Department. They took out my file card and said: 'Hm.' I also said: 'Hm.'

'Which leg?' asked the official.

'The right.'

'The whole leg?'

'The whole leg.'

'Hm,' he went again. He proceeded to shuffle through various papers. I was allowed to sit down.

Finally the man found what seemed to be the right paper. He said: 'I think I have something here for you. Very nice too. A job you can sit down at. Shoeshine stand in a public convenience on Republic Square. How about that?'

'I can't shine shoes; that's one thing people have always noticed about me, my inability to shine shoes.'

'You can learn,' he said. 'One can learn anything. A German can do anything. You can take a free course if you like.'

'Hm,' I went.

'You'll take the job?'

'No,' I said, 'I won't. I want a higher pension.'

'You must be out of your mind,' he replied, his tone mild and good-humoured.

'I'm not out of my mind, no one can give me back my leg, I'm not even allowed to sell cigarettes any more, they're already making that difficult for me.'

The man leaned all the way back in his chair and drew a deep breath. 'My dear fellow,' he said, launching into a lecture, 'your leg's a damned expensive leg. I see that you're twenty-nine years of age, your heart is sound, in fact apart from your leg you're as fit as a fiddle. You'll live to be seventy. Figure it out for yourself, seventy marks a month, twelve times a year, that's forty-one times twelve times seventy. Figure it out for yourself, not counting interest, and don't imagine your leg's unique. What's more, you're not the only one who'll probably live to a ripe old age. And then you want a higher pension! I'm sorry, but you must be out of your mind.'

'I think, sir,' I said, also leaning back and drawing a deep breath, 'I think that you grossly underestimate my leg. My leg is much more expensive, it is a very expensive leg indeed. It so happens that my head is as sound as my heart. Let me explain.'

'I'm a very busy man.'

'I'll explain!' I said. 'You will see that my leg has saved the lives of a great number of people who today are drawing nice fat pensions.

'What happened was this: I was lying all by myself somewhere up front. My job was to spot them when they came so that the others would have time to clear out. The staffs in the rear were packing up, and while they didn't want to clear out too soon they also didn't want to leave it too long. At first there were two of us, but they shot the other fellow, he's not costing you a cent now. It's true he was married, but his wife is in good health and able to work, you don't need to worry. He was a real bargain. He'd only been a soldier for a month, all he cost was a postcard and a few bread rations. There's a good soldier for you, at least he let himself be killed off. But now there I was, all by myself, scared stiff, and it was cold, and I wanted to clear out too, in fact I was just going to clear out when . . .'

'I'm really very busy,' said the man, beginning to search for a pencil.

'No, listen,' I said, 'this is where it gets interesting. Just as I was going to clear out, this business of my leg happened. And because I had to go on lying there anyway, I thought I might as well pass the word, so I passed the word, and they all scrammed, one after another, in descending order of rank, first the divisional staff, then the regimental, then the battalion, and so on, one after another. The silly part was, you see, they were in such a hurry they forgot to take me along! It was really too silly for words, because if I hadn't lost my leg they would all be dead, the general, the colonel, the major, and so on down, and you wouldn't have to pay them any pensions. Now just figure out what my leg is costing you. The general is fifty-two, the colonel forty-eight, and the major fifty, all of them hale and hearty, their heads as well as their hearts, and with the military life they lead they'll live to be at least eighty, like Hindenburg. Figure it out for yourself: a hundred and sixty times twelve times thirty, we'll call it an average of thirty, shall we? My leg's become a damned expensive leg, one of the most expensive legs I can think of, d'you see what I mean?'

'You really must be out of your mind,' said the man.

'No,' I replied, 'I'm not. Unfortunately my heart is as sound as my head, and it's a pity I wasn't killed too, a couple of minutes before that business of my leg happened. We would have saved a lot of money.'

'Are you going to take that job?' asked the man.

'No,' I said, and left.

Lohengrin's Death

Going up the stairs, the men carrying the stretcher slowed down
a bit. They were both feeling resentful, they had been on duty
for over an hour and so far nobody had given them a cigarette for
a tip; besides, one of them was the ambulance driver, and drivers
are not actually required to carry stretchers. But the hospital
hadn't sent anyone down to help, and they couldn't very well
leave the boy lying there in the ambulance; they still had an
emergency pneumonia to pick up and a suicide who had been
cut down at the last minute. They were feeling resentful, and
suddenly they were carrying the stretcher along less slowly
again: the corridor was poorly lit, and of course it smelled of
hospital.

'I wonder why they cut him down?' muttered one of the men,
referring to the suicide; he was the one behind, and the one in
front growled over his shoulder: 'Yeah, why would they do that?'
But because he had turned round as he spoke, he collided with
the doorpost, and the figure lying on the stretcher woke up and
emitted shrill, terrible screams; they were the screams of a child.

'Easy now, easy,' said the doctor, a young interne with fair
hair and a tense face. He looked at the time: eight o'clock, his
relief should have been here long ago. For over an hour he had
been waiting for Dr Lohmeyer: they might have arrested him,
anyone could be arrested any time these days. The young doctor
automatically fingered his stethoscope, his eyes fixed on the boy
on the stretcher, and now for the first time he noticed the
stretcher-bearers standing impatiently by the door. 'What's the
matter, what are you waiting for?' he asked irritably.

131

'The stretcher,' said the driver. 'Can't you move him onto something else? We've got work to do.'

'Oh, of course – over here!' The doctor pointed to the leather couch. At that moment the night nurse appeared, her expression unemotional but serious. She took hold of the boy by the shoulders, and one of the stretcher-bearers, not the driver, grabbed him by the legs.

The boy screamed like one demented, and the doctor said hastily, 'Take it easy now, it's not that bad . . .'

The stretcher-bearers were still standing there, waiting. The doctor's look of annoyance evoked a further response from one of them. 'The blanket,' he said stonily. The blanket wasn't his at all, a woman at the scene of the accident had let him have it, saying they couldn't drive the boy like that to the hospital with those shattered legs of his. But the stretcher-bearer figured the hospital would keep it, and the hospital had plenty of blankets, and the blanket certainly wouldn't be returned to the woman, and it didn't belong to the boy any more than it did to the hospital, and the hospital had plenty. His wife would clean up the blanket all right, and blankets were worth a lot of money these days.

The child was still screaming. They had unwrapped the blanket from around his legs and passed it quickly to the driver. Doctor and nurse exchanged glances. The boy was an appalling sight: the whole lower part of his body was bathed in blood, his cotton shorts were mere shreds, and the shreds had coagulated with the blood into a revolting pulp. His feet were bare, and he screamed without pause, screamed with terrible persistence and regularity.

'Quick,' whispered the doctor, 'a hypo, Nurse, hurry, please!' The nurse's movements were skilful and swift, but the doctor kept whispering: 'Hurry, hurry!' His mouth hung slack in his tense face. The boy kept up his incessant screaming, but the the nurse was preparing the hypo as fast as she could.

The doctor felt the boy's pulse, his pale face twitching with exhaustion. 'Be quiet,' he whispered a few times distraughtly, 'be *quiet*!' But the child screamed as if he had been born for the sole purpose of screaming. At last the nurse brought the hypo, and the doctor swiftly and skilfully gave the injection.

With a sigh he drew the needle out of the tough, leathery skin, and just then the door opened and a nun burst into the room, but when she saw the accident case and the doctor she closed her mouth, which she had opened, and approached slowly and quietly. She gave the doctor and the pale lay-sister a friendly nod and placed her hand on the child's forehead. The boy opened his eyes and looked straight up, in surprise, at the black figure standing behind him. It seemed almost as if the pressure of the cool hand on his brow were quieting him down, but the injection was already taking effect. The doctor was still holding the syringe, and he gave another deep sigh, for it was quiet now, blissfully quiet, so quiet that they could all hear their own breathing. They did not speak.

The boy was evidently out of pain now; he was looking quietly and interestedly around the room.

'How much?' the doctor asked the night nurse in a low voice.

'Ten,' she replied, in the same tone.

The doctor shrugged his shoulders' 'Quite a bit, we'll see what happens. Would you give us a hand, Sister Lioba?'

'Of course,' the nun replied promptly, seeming to rouse herself from a deep reverie. It was very quiet. The nun held the boy by the head and shoulders, the night nurse took his legs, and together they pulled off the blood-soaked tatters. The blood, as they now saw, was mixed with something black; everything was black, the boy's feet were caked with coal dust, his hands too, there was nothing but blood, shreds of cloth, and coal dust, thick oily coal dust.

'Obviously,' murmured the doctor, 'you fell off a moving train while pinching coal, eh?'

'Yes,' said the boy in a cracked voice, 'obviously.'

His eyes were wide open, and there was a strange happiness in them. The injection must have been gloriously effective. The nun pulled his shirt all the way up, arranging it in a roll on the boy's chest, under his chin. His chest was scrawny, ludicrously scrawny like the breast of an elderly goose. Alongside the collar bones strangely deep shadows filled the hollows, great cavities where she could have hidden the whole of her broad white hand. Now they could see his legs too, as much of them as was still intact. They were skinny, and seemed to be fine-boned and shapely. The doctor nodded to the women, saying: 'Double fracture of both legs, I imagine; we'll need an X-ray.'

The night nurse wiped his legs clean with alcohol, and now they didn't look quite so bad. But the child was so appallingly thin. The doctor shook his head as he applied the bandage. He started worrying again about Lohmeyer, maybe they'd got him after all, and even if he kept his mouth shut it was still very awkward to let him take the rap for that Strophanthin business and get off scot-free himself, while if things had gone well he would have had a share in the profits. Hell, it must be eight-thirty, it was ominously quiet now, not a sound from the street. He had finished his bandaging, and the nun pulled the boy's shirt down again over his loins. Then she went to the closet, took out a white blanket, and spread it over the boy.

Her hands on the boy's forehead again, she said to the doctor as he was washing his hands: 'What I really came about was the little Schranz girl, Doctor, but I didn't want to worry you while you were treating this boy.'

The doctor paused in his drying, made a slight grimace, and the cigarette hanging from his lower lip quivered.

'Well,' he asked, 'what about the Schranz child?'

The pallor in his face was almost yellow now.

'I'm afraid that little heart is giving up, just giving up, it looks like the end.'

The doctor took the cigarette between his fingers again and hung the towel on the nail beside the washbowl.

'Hell,' he cried helplessly, 'what am I supposed to do? There's nothing I can do!'

The nun kept her hand on the boy's forehead. The night nurse dropped the blood-soaked rags into the garbage pail; its chrome lid cast flickering lights against the wall.

The doctor stood there thinking, his eyes lowered. Suddenly he raised his head, gave one more look at the boy, and dashed to the door: 'I'll have a look at her.'

'Do you need me?' the night nurse called out after him. He put his head in again, saying:

'No, you stay here, get the boy ready for X-rays and see if you can take down his history.'

The boy was still very quiet, and the night nurse came and stood by the leather couch.

'Has your mother been told?' asked the nun.

'She's dead.'

The nurse did not dare ask about his father.

'Whom should we notify?'

'My older brother, only he's not home right now. But the kids ought to be told, they're all alone now.'

'What kids?'

'Hans and Adolf, they're waiting for me to come and get supper.'

'And where does your older brother work?'

The boy was silent, and the nun did not pursue the question.

'Would you mind taking it down, Nurse?'

The night nurse nodded and went over to the little white table that was covered with medicine bottles and test tubes. She pulled the ink towards her, dipped the pen in it, and smoothed out the sheet of white paper with her left hand.

'What's your name?' the nun asked the boy.

'Becker.'

'Religion?'

'None. I was never baptized.'

The nun winced, the night nurse's expression remained impassive.

'When were you born?'

'1933 . . . September tenth.'

'Still going to school, I suppose?'

'Yes.'

'And . . . his first name!' the night nurse whispered to the nun.

'Oh yes . . . and your first name?'

'Grini.'

'What?' The two women looked at each other and smiled.

'Grini,' said the boy, slowly and peevishly, as anyone does who has an unusual first name.

'With an i?' asked the night nurse.

'That's right, with two i's,' and he repeated once more: 'Grini.'

His real name was Lohengrin, he had been born in 1933 just when the first photographs of Hitler at the Bayreuth Wagner Festival started flooding all the illustrated weeklies. But his mother had always called him Grini.

The doctor rushed suddenly into the room, his eyes blurred with exhaustion, his wispy fair hair hanging down into his young, deeply lined face.

'Come along, both of you, and be quick about it. I'm going to try a transfusion, hurry up!'

The nun's eyes went to the boy.

'That's all right,' cried the doctor, 'you can leave him alone for a moment.'

The night nurse was already at the door.

'Will you lie there quietly like a good boy, Grini?' asked the nun.

'Yes,' he answered.

But as soon as they had all left the room he let the tears flow unchecked. It was as if the nun's hand on his brow had held them back. He was crying not with pain but with happiness. And yet with pain and fear too. It was only when he thought about the kids that he cried with pain, and he tried not to think about them because he wanted to cry with happiness. Never in his life had he had such a wonderful feeling as now, after the injection. It flowed right through him like some wonderful, gently warmed milk, making him feel dizzy and yet awake, and

there was a delicious taste on his tongue, more delicious than
anything he had ever tasted, but he couldn't help it, he kept
thinking about the kids. Hubert wouldn't be back before tomorrow morning, and Father, of course, wouldn't be home for
another three weeks, and Mother . . . and right now the kids
were waiting all alone, and he knew very well that they listened
for every step, every tiny sound on the stairs, and there were so
many, many sounds on the stairs, and the kids were disappointed
so many, many times. There wasn't much hope that Frau
Grossmann would bother about them: she never had, why should
she today, she never had, and after all she couldn't know that
he . . . that he had had an accident. Hans might try to comfort
Adolf, but Hans was so frail himself and the least thing made
him cry. Maybe Adolf would comfort Hans, but Adolf was only
five whereas Hans was eight, it was really more likely that Hans
would comfort Adolf. But Hans was so terribly frail, and Adolf
was much stronger. Probably they would both cry, for when it
got close to seven o'clock they would tire of playing because they
were hungry and knew he would be home at seven-thirty and
give them something to eat. And they wouldn't dare take any
of the bread; no, they would never dare do that again, he had
forbidden them too strictly since those few times when they had
eaten it all up, every bit, the whole week's rations; it wouldn't
matter if they took some of the potatoes, but of course they didn't
know that. If only he had told them it was all right to take some
of the potatoes. Hans was already quite good at boiling them;
but they wouldn't dare, he had punished them too severely, in
fact he had even had to hit them, for it just wouldn't do for them
to eat up all the bread; it just wouldn't do, but now he would
have been glad if he hadn't punished them, for then they would
take some of the bread and at least they wouldn't be hungry. So
instead they were sitting there waiting, and at every sound on
the stairs they were jumping up excitedly and thrusting their
pale faces through the crack of the door, the way he had seen
them so often, a thousand times maybe. Oh, he always saw their
faces first, and they were glad to see him. Yes, even after he had

137

hit them, they were glad to see him; they had understood, he knew that. And now every sound was a disappointment, and they would be scared. Hans trembled at the very sight of a policeman; maybe they'd make such a noise crying that Frau Grossmann would be angry, for she liked peace and quiet of an evening, and then maybe they would go on crying, and Frau Grossmann would come and see what was the matter and take pity on them; she wasn't so bad, Frau Grossmann. But Hans would never go on his own to Frau Grossmann, he was so dreadfully scared of her, Hans was scared of everything . . .

If only they would take some of the potatoes at least!

Now that he had begun thinking about the kids, he was crying with pain. He tried holding his hand in front of his eyes so as not to see the kids, but he felt his hand getting wet, and he cried even more. He tried to figure out the time. It must be nine o'clock, maybe ten, that was terrible. He had never got home later than seven-thirty, but today the train had been closely watched and they had had to keep a sharp lookout, those Luxembourgers were so trigger-happy. Maybe during the war they hadn't been able to shoot much and they just enjoyed shooting; but they didn't get him, oh no, they'd never got him, he'd always given them the slip. Anthracite, people would pay seventy to eighty marks for anthracite and think nothing of it; and he was supposed to miss a chance like that? But those Luxembourgers had never got him, he'd managed to cope with the Russians, with the Yanks, and the Tommies, and the Belgians, was he going to let himself get caught by the Luxembourgers of all people, those clowns? He had slipped past them, up onto the train, filled his sack, tossed it down, and then thrown down whatever he still had time to lay hands on. But then, crash, the train had stopped with a sudden jolt, and he knew nothing except that he had been in the most frightful agony until he knew nothing whatever, and then there had been the pain again when he woke up in the doorway and saw the white room. And then they had given him the injection. Now he was crying with happiness again. The kids had gone; this happiness was glorious, he had never known such bliss; his tears seemed to be bliss itself, bliss was flowing out of him, and yet it didn't get any smaller, this flickering, exquisite, circling thing in his chest, this funny lump that welled up out of him in tears, didn't get any smaller . . .

Suddenly he heard the Luxembourgers shooting, they had machine pistols, and it made a horrible racket in the cool spring evening; there was a smell of fields, smoke from the station, coal, and even a bit of real spring. Two shots barked into the sky, which was dark grey, and the echo of them returned to him a thousand times over, and there was a prickling in his chest like pins and needles; those damned Luxembourgers weren't going to get him, they weren't going to shoot him to bits! The coal he was lying on was hard and sharp, it was anthracite, and they paid eighty marks, up to eighty marks a hundredweight for it. Should he get the kids some chocolate? No, it wouldn't be enough, for chocolate they wanted forty marks, sometimes forty-five. He couldn't carry away that much: God, he'd have to lug a whole hundredweight for two bars of chocolate; and those Luxembourgers were crazy nuts, now they'd started shooting again, and his bare feet were cold and the sharp anthracite hurt them, and they were black and dirty, he could feel it. The shots were tearing great holes in the sky, but surely they couldn't shoot the sky to bits, or maybe the Luxembourgers could shoot the sky to bits . . . ?

Would he have to tell the nurse where his father was and where Hubert went at night? They hadn't asked him, and it was better not to answer unless you were asked. They'd told him in school . . . damn those Luxembourgers . . . and the kids . . . the Luxembourgers ought to stop shooting, he had to get to the kids . . . they must be crazy, completely out of their minds, those Luxembourgers. Hell no, he wasn't going to tell the nurse where their father was and where their brother went at night, and maybe the kids would take some of the bread after all . . . or some of the potatoes . . . or maybe Frau Grossmann would notice there was something wrong, for there was something wrong: it was funny, there was always something wrong. The principal would bawl him out at school too. The injection had been wonderful, he

139

could feel the prick, and suddenly there was that bliss! That pale-faced nurse had filled the needle with bliss, and he'd heard them all right, he'd heard that she had filled the needle with too much bliss, much too much bliss, he was no fool. Grini with two i's . . . nonsense, he's dead . . . no, missing. This bliss was glorious, one day he'd buy the bliss in the needle for the kids; you could buy anything . . . bread . . . whole mountains of bread . . .

Hell, with two i's, don't these people know a good German name when they hear it . . . ?

'None,' he shouted suddenly, 'I was never baptized!'

Maybe their mother was still alive after all? No, the Luxembourgers had shot her, no the Russians . . . no, who knows, maybe the Nazis had shot her, she had got so terribly mad at them . . . no, the Yanks . . . for God's sake, what did it matter if the kids ate the bread, ate the bread . . . a whole mountain of bread, that's what he'd buy the kids . . . bread piled up to the sky . . . a whole boxcar full of bread . . . full of anthracite; and bliss in the needle.

With two i's, damn it!

The nun hurried over to him, felt at once for his pulse, and looked round in alarm. Dear God, ought she to call the doctor? But she couldn't leave the delirious child alone now. The little Schranz girl was dead, gone, thank God, that child with the Russian face! Why didn't the doctor come . . . she ran round behind the leather couch . . .

'None,' shouted the child, 'I was never baptized!'

His pulse was getting wilder and wilder every moment. Sweat stood out on the nun's forehead. 'Doctor, Doctor!' she called, but she knew quite well that no sound penetrated the padded door.

The child was now whimpering pitifully.

'Bread . . . a whole mountain of bread for the kids . . . chocolate . . . anthracite . . . the Luxembourgers, those swine, they oughtn't to shoot, damn it, the potatoes, sure you can take some of the potatoes . . . go ahead, take some! Frau Grossmann . . . Father . . .

Mother . . . Hubert . . . through the crack in the door, through the crack in the door.'

The nun was weeping with anguish, she dared not leave, the child was beginning to thrash about and she held onto him by the shoulders. The leather couch was so horribly slippery. The little Schranz girl was dead, that little heart was in Heaven. God have mercy on her; dear God, mercy . . . she was innocent, a little angel, an ugly little Russian angel . . . but now she was pretty . . .

'None,' shouted the boy, trying to flail around with his arms, 'I was never baptized!'

The nun looked up in dismay. She ran to the sink, keeping an anxious eye on the boy, but there was no glass, she ran back, stroked the feverish forehead. Then she went over to the little white table and picked up a test tube. The test tube was soon full, it doesn't take much water to fill a test tube . . .

'Bliss,' whispered the child, 'fill the needle with lots of bliss, all you've got, for the kids too . . .'

The nun crossed herself solemnly, deliberately, then sprinkled the water from the test tube over the boy's forehead, saying through her tears: 'I baptize thee . . .' but the boy, suddenly sobered by the cold water, jerked up his head so violently that the tube fell from the nun's hand and smashed on the floor. The boy looked at the startled nun with a little smile and said feebly: 'Baptize . . . yes . . .' then he dropped back so abruptly that his head fell on the leather couch with a dull thud, and now his face looked narrow and old, frighteningly yellow, as he lay there motionless, his fingers spread to grasp . . .

'Has he been X-rayed yet?' cried the doctor, chuckling as he came into the room with Dr Lohmeyer. The nun merely shook her head. The doctor stepped closer, felt automatically for his stethoscope, but dropped it and looked at Lohmeyer. Lohmeyer removed his hat. Lohengrin was dead . . .

Business is Business

My black marketeer is an honest citizen these days; it was a long time since I had seen him, months in fact, and today I came across him in quite a different part of the city, at a busy intersection. He has a wooden booth there now, all done up in the best white paint; a handsome corrugated iron roof, solid and brand-new, shields him from rain and cold, and he sells cigarettes and all-day suckers, quite legally. At first I was pleased; it is always nice, after all, to see someone find his way back to normal life. For when we first met, things were going badly for him, and we were depressed. We still went around in our old army caps, and whenever I came by some cash I used to go and see him, and we would have a chat, about being hungry, about the war; and now and again, when I didn't have any money, he would give me a cigarette, or I would take along some bread-ration coupons as I happened to be clearing rubble for a baker at the time.

He seemed to be doing all right now. He looked the picture of health. His cheeks had that firmness that comes only from a regular intake of fats, his expression was self-confident, and I watched him bawl out a grubby little girl and send her packing because she was short five pfennigs for an all-day sucker. And all the time he kept feeling around in his mouth with his tongue as if he were forever trying to pry shreds of meat from between his teeth.

Business was brisk; they were buying a lot of cigarettes from him, and all-day suckers as well.

Maybe I shouldn't have – I went up to him and said 'Ernst,' intending to have a word with him.

He was very surprised, gave me an odd look and said: 'What's that?' I could see he recognized me but that he wasn't too keen on being recognized.

I was silent. I behaved as if I had never said Ernst to him, bought some cigarettes, since I happened to have some cash, and left. I watched him a while longer; my streetcar wasn't in sight yet, and I didn't feel in the least like going home. At home I'm always being pestered by people wanting money; my landlady asking for the rent, and the man with the electricity bill. Besides, I'm not allowed to smoke at home; my landlady always manages to smell it, she gets mad and I'm told that I seem to have money for tobacco but none for the rent. It's a sin, you see, for the poor to smoke or drink. I know it's a sin, that's why I do it secretly, I smoke outdoors, and just occasionally when I'm lying awake and everything is quiet, when I know that by morning the smell will have disappeared, then I smoke in my room too.

The terrible thing is that I have no profession. For you have to have a profession. That's what they tell you. There was a time when they used to say it was unnecessary, all we needed was soldiers. But now they say you have to have a profession. Just like that. They say you are lazy when you don't have a profession. But that's not so. I'm not lazy, but the jobs they give me are jobs I don't want to do. Clearing rubble and carrying rocks, and things like that. After two hours I'm soaked with sweat, everything becomes a blur, and when I go to the doctors they tell me there's nothing wrong. Maybe it's nerves. Nowadays they talk a lot about nerves. But I believe it's a sin for the poor to have nerves. To be poor and to have nerves, that seems to be more than they can stand. But my nerves are all shot, I can tell you that; I was a soldier too long. Nine years, I think. Maybe more, I'm not sure. Once upon a time I would have been glad to have a profession, I wanted very much to go into business. But once upon a time – what's the use of talking about it; now I don't even feel like going into business any more. What I like to do best is lie on my bed and daydream. I figure out how many hundreds of thousands of man-hours they need to build a bridge or a big house and then I think that in a single minute they can smash both the bridge and the house. So what's the point of working? To my mind there's no sense in working. I think that's what drives me crazy when I have to carry rocks or clear rubble so they can build another café.

A minute ago I was saying it was nerves, but I think that's the real reason: it's all so senseless.

Actually I don't care what they think. But it's terrible never to have any money. You've simply got to have money. You can't get along without it. There's a meter, and you have a lamp, naturally you need light sometimes, you switch it on, and right away the money's pouring out of the light bulb. Even when you don't need any light you have to pay rent for the meter. That's the whole trouble: rent. It seems you've got to have a room. At first I lived in a cellar, it wasn't too bad down there, I had a stove and used to pinch briquettes; but they unearthed me, they came from the newspaper, took my picture, wrote an article to go with the picture: RETURNING VETERAN LIVES IN POVERTY. I had to move, that's all there was to it. The man from the housing office said it was a matter of prestige for him and I had to take the room. Sometimes, of course, I make some money. Obviously. I run errands, deliver briquettes and stack them up nice and neatly in a corner of someone's cellar. I am very good at stacking briquettes, I don't charge much either. Needless to say I don't earn much, it's never enough for the rent, sometimes it's enough for the electricity, a few cigarettes and bread . . .

I was thinking of all this as I stood at the corner.

My black marketeer, who is now an honest citizen, threw me a suspicious look from time to time. That bastard knows perfectly well who I am, people do know each other, after all, when they've spoken to one another almost every day for two years. Maybe he thought I was going to pinch something. I'm not as dumb as all that, to pinch something at a busy spot with streetcars stopping every minute and even a cop standing at the corner. I pinch things in quite different places: naturally I pinch things sometimes, things like coal. Wood too. The other day I even pinched a loaf in a bakery. You wouldn't believe how quick and easy it was. I just took the loaf and walked out, I walked along quite calmly, as far as the next corner, then I started to run. I've lost the nerve I used to have, that's all.

I certainly wouldn't pinch anything at a corner like that, although sometimes it's easy, but I've lost my nerve. Several streetcars stopped, including my own, and I could see Ernst looking sidelong at me when mine came up. That bastard still remembers which is my streetcar!

But I threw away the butt of my first cigarette, lit another, and stayed where I was. I've progressed that far, at least, that I throw away butts. Yet over there someone was creeping around picking up butts, and you have to think of the other fellow. There are still some people who pick up cigarette butts. They aren't always the same ones. In the P.O.W. camp I had seen colonels doing it, but this one wasn't a colonel. I watched him. He had his own system, like a spider lurking in its web he had his headquarters somewhere in a pile of rubble, and whenever a streetcar stopped or started up he would emerge and walk unhurriedly along the curb collecting the butts. I would have liked to go up to him and speak to him, I feel we are two of a kind: but I know it's no use; those fellows never say anything.

I don't know what was the matter with me, but that day I just didn't want to go home. The very word: home. I was past caring now, I let one more streetcar go by and lighted another cigarette. I don't know what's wrong with us. Maybe some professor will find out one day and write an article about it in the paper; they have an explanation for everything. I only wish I still had the nerve to pinch things, like I did in the war. In those days it used to be quick and easy. In those days, during the war, when there was anything to be pinched it was we who had to go out and pinch it; they used to say: don't worry, he knows how to do it, and off we would go to pinch something. The others just helped eat and drink up the stuff, send it home and all that, but they didn't pinch anything. Their nerves were in perfect shape, and they managed to keep their copybooks clean.

And when we came home they got out of the war as if they

were getting out of a streetcar that happened to slow down just where they lived, and they jumped off without paying the fare. They turned aside, went indoors, and lo and behold: the dresser was still standing, there was a little dust on the bookshelves, your wife had potatoes stored in the cellar, and some preserves; you embraced her a bit, as was right and proper, and next morning you went off to find out whether your job was still open: the job was still open. Everything was fine, your medical insurance was still okay, you had yourself denazified a bit – the way you go to the barber to get rid of that tiresome beard – you chatted about decorations, wounds, acts of heroism, and came to the conclusion you were a pretty fine fellow after all: you had simply done your duty. There were weekly streetcar passes again, the best sign that everything was back to normal.

Meanwhile the rest of us stayed on the streetcar and waited to see if somewhere there would be a stop that seemed familiar enough for us to risk getting off: it never came. Some people went on a bit farther, but they jumped off somewhere too, trying to look as if they had reached their destination.

But we went on and on, the fare went up automatically, and we had to pay for our bulky heavy baggage as well: for the leaden mass of nothingness that we had to lug around with us; and first one inspector got on, then another, and we would shrug our shoulders and show them our empty pockets. They couldn't throw us off, the streetcar was going too fast – 'and we were human beings after all' – but they wrote down our names, over and over again they wrote down our names, the streetcar went faster and faster; the smart ones jumped off quickly, anywhere, fewer and fewer of us stayed on, and fewer and fewer of us had the guts or the desire to get off. At the back of our minds we meant to leave our baggage on the streetcar, to let the Lost and Found auction it off as soon as we reached the terminus; but the terminus never came, the fare went up and up, the streetcar went faster and faster, the inspectors got more and more sceptical, we are a highly suspect lot.

I threw away the butt of my third cigarette and walked slowly across to the streetcar stop; I wanted to go home now. I felt dizzy: one shouldn't smoke so much on an empty stomach, I know that. I quit looking over to where my former black marketeer was now carrying on a legitimate business; I really have no right to be angry; he made it, he jumped off, probably at the right moment, but I don't know whether it's all right for him to bawl out kids who are short five pfennigs for an all-day sucker. Maybe that's all part of legitimate business: I wouldn't know.

Just before my streetcar arrived, the bum walked unhurriedly along the curb again, in front of the ranks of waiting people, to collect butts. They don't like to see that, I know. They would rather it wasn't that way, but that's the way it is . . .

I didn't look at Ernst again until I was on the streetcar, but he glanced away and shouted: 'Chocolate, candy, cigarettes, all ration-free!' I don't know what's wrong, but I must say I liked him better before, when he didn't need to send anyone away who was short five pfennigs; but now of course he has a proper business, and business is business.

On the Hook

I know it's stupid. I ought to stop going there; it's so senseless, yet going there is what keeps me alive. A single minute of hope and twenty-three hours and fifty-nine minutes of despair. That's what keeps me alive. It's not much, there's precious little substance to it. I ought to stop going there. It's killing me, that's what: it's killing me. But I've got to go, I've got to, I've got to ...

The train she's supposed to arrive on is always the same one, the one-twenty PM. The train always pulls in on time, I keep a sharp eye on everything, they can't fool me.

The man with the baton is always ready for me when I turn up; when he comes out of his little signal house – I've already heard the signal bell ringing inside it – as I say, when he comes out, I go over to him, he knows me by this time: he puts on a sympathetic expression, sympathetic and a bit scared; yes, the man with the baton is scared; maybe he thinks I'll go for him one day; I might at that, one of these days, I might beat him up, kill him, and dump his body between the tracks to be run over by the one-twenty. You see, that man with the baton – I don't trust him. I don't know whether his pity is an act or not; maybe it's just an act. He's scared all right, that's genuine enough, and he has good reason to be: one day I'll beat his brains out with his own baton. I don't trust him, maybe he's in cahoots with them. After all, he does have a phone in his signal house – all he has to do is crank the handle and call them up – those railway jokers get through in a second: maybe he lifts the receiver, phones the last-but-one station and tells them: 'Take her off the train, arrest her; don't let her get back on ... what? ... that's right, the woman with the brown hair and the little green hat; yes, that's the one, hold on to her' – then he laughs – 'that's right, that nut's here again, we'll let him wait for nothing again. Be sure you hold on to her now.'

He hangs up and laughs; then he comes out, puts on his pitying expression when he sees me shuffling over to him, and says, as he always does even before I ask him: 'Right on time again, sir, same as usual!'

This not knowing whether I can trust him is driving me crazy. Perhaps he grins the moment he turns his back on me. He always does turn his back on me and acts as if he had something important to do, like on the platform; he walks up and down, waves people back from the edge of the platform, finds all sorts of things to do that are quite superfluous, for the people step back from the edge anyway as soon as they see him coming. He's just putting on a show, pretending to be busy, and perhaps he grins the moment he turns his back. Once I wanted to test him – I darted round in front of him and looked him straight in the face. But there was nothing there to confirm my suspicions : only fear . . .

All the same, I don't trust him, those fellows have more self-control than our sort; they're capable of anything. It's a kind of clique that's got strength and security, while we – the ones who wait – have nothing. We live on a razor's edge, balancing from one minute of hope to the next minute of hope. For twenty-three hours and fifty-nine minutes we balance on the razor's edge, one minute's respite is all we get. They have us on a tight rein, those fellows, those jokers with their batons, those stinkers, they call each other up, exchange a couple of words, and our life is down the drain again, down the drain again for twenty-three hours and fifty-nine minutes. They're the ones who run the show, those bastards . . .

His pity is an act, I'm quite sure of that now. When I really think about it, I have to acknowledge that he's double-crossing me. They're all crooks. They're holding on to her; I know she meant to come, she told me so in a letter: 'I love you, and I'm coming on the one-twenty PM.' Arriving one-twenty PM., she wrote, that was three months ago, three months and four days exactly. They're keeping her back, they don't want us to meet, they begrudge me the chance of ever having more than one minute's hope, let alone joy. They're preventing our rendezvous; somewhere or other they're sitting and laughing, they're all in it together. They laugh and call each other up, and that stinker with the baton gets paid, and well paid too, for telling me day after day, in that mealy-mouthed way of his: 'Right on time again, sir, same as usual!' Even the 'sir' is an insult. No one ever calls me 'sir', I'm a poor down-and-out bastard who lives on one minute of hope a day. That's all. No one ever calls me 'sir', shit on his 'sir'. They can do it to me backwards but they've got to let her go, let her get back on that train; they've got to give her to me, she's mine, didn't she send me a telegram, 'I love you, arriving there one-twenty PM.'? 'There' means where I live. That's what telegrams are like: you write 'there', and you mean the town where the other person lives. 'Arriving there one-twenty PM.' . . .

Today I'm going to do him in, I'm about ready to blow my top. My patience is exhausted, my strength too. I'm at the end of my tether. If I see him today, he's had it. It's been going on too long. Besides, I've no more money. No more money for the streetcar. I've already flogged everything I own. For three months and four days I've been living off capital. I've flogged the lot, even the tablecloth; I can't kid myself anymore – today there's nothing left. There's just enough for one streetcar ride. Not even enough for the return trip, I'll have to walk back . . . or . . . or . . .

In any case that bastard with the baton will be lying down there between the tracks, a bloody mess, and the one-twenty will run over him, he'll be wiped out, just as I'll be wiped out this afternoon at one-twenty . . . or . . . Christ!

It's really too much when you don't even have money for the return trip; they make things too hard for a man. The clique sticks together, they control hope, they control paradise, consolation. They've got their talons round everything. We're only allowed to nibble at it, for a single minute a day. For twenty-three hours and fifty-nine minutes we have to hanker after it, lie in wait for it; they even refuse to dole out the artificial paradises. And they don't even need them; I wonder why they hang on to everything? Is it just for the sake of the money? Why don't they ever give a man money for booze or smokes, why do they put such a terrible price on consolation? They keep us dangling on the hook, and every time we bite, every time we let ourselves be pulled up to the surface, every time we breathe light, beauty, joy for one minute, some bastard laughs, slackens the line, and there we are back in the dark . . .

They make things too hard for us; today I'm going to have my revenge. I'm going to take that stinker with the baton, that outpost of security, and dump him between the tracks. Maybe that'll give them a fright, sitting back there by their phones – Christ, if only a fellow could frighten them, just once! But you haven't a chance, that's the trouble; they hold on to everything, bread, wine, tobacco, they've got the lot, and they've got her too: 'Arriving there one-twenty PM.' No date. That's the trouble: she never writes the date.

They're jealous because I might have kissed her; no, no, no, we have to perish, suffocate, despair utterly, go without consolation, flog everything we own, and when we've nothing left we have to . . .

For that's the terrible part about it: the minute is shrinking. I've noticed it the last few days: the minute is shrinking. I think it may be only thirty seconds now, perhaps much less, I don't even dare work out how much really is left. Yesterday, anyway, I noticed it was less. Up till then, whenever the train came in sight round the curve, black and snorting against the city's spreading horizon, I was always conscious of being happy. She's coming, I used to think, she's got through, she's coming! I would go on thinking that the whole time, till the train came to a halt, the people got slowly out – the platform gradually emptied . . . and . . . nothing . . .

No, then I wasn't thinking that any more. I must try above all to be honest with myself. When the first people got out and she wasn't among them, I wasn't thinking that any more, it was all over. That happiness – it wasn't that it stopped sooner, it began later. That's how it was. One must be honest and objective about it. It began later, that's how it was. It used to begin when the train came in sight, black and snorting against the city's spreading horizon; yesterday it didn't begin until the train had come to a halt. When it had stopped moving altogether, when it was just standing there, that's when I began to hope; and when it was standing there, the doors were already opening . . . and she didn't come . . .

Now I'm wondering whether that lasted even thirty seconds. I haven't the nerve to be quite honest and say: it's only one second . . . and twenty-three hours, fifty-nine minutes, and fifty-nine seconds of black darkness . . .

I haven't the nerve; I can scarcely bring myself to go back there; it would be too horrible if not even this second were left. Are they going to take that away from me too?

It's too little. There are limits. A certain amount of substance is needed by even the lowliest of creatures, even the lowliest of creatures needs at least one second a day. They mustn't take this one second away from me, they're making it too short.

Their callousness is assuming terrible forms. Now I don't even have the money for the return trip. Not even for the fare straight there and back, let alone transfer, as I have to. I'm short exactly a nickel. Their callousness is cruel. They've even stopped buying. They don't even want to buy things now. Until now they've always been screaming to buy things. But now their greed has become so appalling that they're sitting on their money and devouring it. I really do believe they devour their money. I wonder what for? What do they want? They've got bread, wine, tobacco, they've got money, everything, they've got their fat women – what else do they want? Why have they stopped shelling out? No money, not an ounce of bread, no tobacco, not a drop of schnapps . . . nothing . . . nothing. They're forcing me to extreme measures.

I shall have to take up the struggle. I'm going to finish off that outpost of theirs, that bastard with his baton and his pitying expression, he screws me every time he talks to them on the phone! He's in cahoots with them, I know that now for certain because yesterday I listened in on him! That bastard's double-crossing me, I'm sure of that now. I went much earlier yesterday, much earlier, he couldn't have known I was there, I ducked down under the window and waited, and sure enough! – he cranked the handle, the bell tinkled, and I heard his voice! 'Superintendent,' he said, 'Superintendent, something's got to be done about it. The fellow can't be allowed to go on like that. After all, the security of a civil servant is at stake! Superintendent,' his voice implored, that bastard really was scared stiff. 'That's right, Platform 4b.'

Very well, so now I've got proof. Now they'll take drastic measures. Now they're really going to finish me off. Now it's a fight to the finish. At least the position is clear. I'm glad of that. I shall fight like a lion. I'll run down the whole lot of them, herd them all together and toss them in front of the one-twenty . . .

Not one thing are they willing to let me keep. They're driving me to desperation, they want to rob me of my last second. And they've even stopped buying. Not even watches, till now they've always been keen on watches. All I got for my books was three pounds of tea – two hundred pretty nice books at that. I imagine they were pretty nice. I used to be very interested in literature. But three pounds of tea for two hundred books – what a lousy deal; the bread I got for the sheets and pillow slips was hardly worth mentioning, my mother's jewellery gave me enough to live on for a month, and you need such a tremendous amount when you live on a razor's edge. Three months and four days is a long time, a fellow needs too much.

As a last resort there's always Father's watch. The watch has a certain value. No one can deny that the watch has a certain value; perhaps it's enough for the return trip; perhaps the conductor has a kind heart and will let me ride back in exchange for the watch; perhaps, perhaps I shall need two tickets for the return trip: Christ!

It's twelve-thirty and I must get ready. That doesn't involve much, nothing at all really; I just have to get out of bed, that's all there is to getting ready. The room is bare, I've flogged everything. A fellow has to live, after all. The landlady has taken the mattress for a month's rent. She's a good sort, a really good sort, one of the best I've ever met. A good woman. A fellow can doss down perfectly well on the wire springs. No one knows how well you can sleep on wire springs, if you sleep at all, that is; I never sleep, I live on capital, I live on one second's hope, on the second when the doors open and no one comes . . .

I must pull myself together, the battle's about to begin. It's a quarter to one, the streetcar passes at ten to, that'll get me to the station on the dot of quarter past, onto the platform by eighteen past; when that joker with the baton comes out of his signal house, I'll be just in time to let him tell me: 'Right on time again, sir, same as usual!'

The bastard really does say 'sir' to me; everyone else he just bawls out, shouting: 'Hey you there – get back from the edge of the platform!' To me he says: 'Sir!' That just shows: it's all a big fake, a horrible big fake; when you look at them you're tempted to think they're hungry too, that they're all out of tea or tobacco or booze; the expression on their faces is enough to make you almost want to flog your last shirt for them.

A fellow could cry for years over the big fake they put on. I must try to cry; it must be wonderful to cry, a substitute for wine, tobacco, bread, and maybe even a substitute for when the single solitary second is extinct and all I have left is twenty-four naked, entire hours of despair.

I can't cry in the streetcar, of course; I must pull myself together, I really must pull myself together. They mustn't notice anything; and at the station I'll have to watch out. I'm sure they have people hidden somewhere. 'After all, the security of a civil servant is at stake, Platform 4b.' I'll have to be damn careful. It makes me nervous the way the conductress keeps looking at me. She asks several times, 'Tickets?', looking only at me: and I really have one; I could pull it out and hold it under her nose, she gave it to me herself, but she's forgotten already. 'Tickets?' she asks three times, looking at me; I blush, I really do have one; she moves on, and everyone thinks: 'He hasn't got one, he's cheating the transit company.' And all the time I've given up my last twenty pfennigs, I've even got a transfer . . .

I must watch out like hell; I very nearly ran through the barrier, like I always do; but they might be standing around any place; as I was just about to dash through I realized I didn't have a platform ticket, or a nickel. It's seventeen minutes past, in three minutes the train will be in. I'm going crazy. 'Take this watch,' I said. The man looks insulted. 'For God's sake, take this watch.' He pushes me back. Their excellencies the ticket-holders are staring. There's no help for it, I have to go back, it's seventeen and a half minutes past.

'A watch!' I shout. 'A watch for a nickel! An honest watch, not a stolen one, a watch that belonged to my father!' Everyone takes me for a nut or a criminal. Not one of those bastards will take my watch. Perhaps they'll call the police. I must find the bums. The bums will help me at least. The bums are all down below. It's eighteen minutes past, I'm going crazy. Am I to miss the train today of all days, the very day she's going to arrive? 'Arriving there one-twenty PM.'

'Hey, buddy,' I say to the first bum I see, 'give me a nickel for this watch, but quick, quick,' I say.

He stares too, even he stares. 'Listen, buddy,' I tell him, 'I've got one more minute, understand?'

He understands, he misunderstands of course, but at least he tries to understand, at least it's something to be misunderstood. At least it's a kind of understanding. The others understand nothing.

He gives me a mark, he's generous. 'Listen, buddy,' I say, 'I need a nickel, get it? Not a mark, understand?'

He misunderstands again, but it's so good to be at least mis-understood; if I get out of this alive I'll hug you, buddy.

He gives me a nickel as well, that's how the bums are, they give a bit extra and at least they misunderstand.

On the Hook

I manage to race up the steps at nineteen and a half minutes past one. But I still have to be on the alert, I have to watch out like crazy. There comes the train, black and snorting against the city's grey horizon. My heart is silent at the sight of it, but I am in time, that's the main thing. In spite of everything, I've managed to get here in time.

I keep well away from the joker with the baton; he is surrounded by people, and suddenly he's caught sight of me, he calls out, he's scared, he waves to the clique hiding in his signal house, waves to them to catch me. They dash out, they've almost got me, but I laugh in their faces, I laugh in their faces, for the train has pulled in and before they get to me she is in my arms, my girl, and all I own in the world is my girl and a platform ticket, my girl and a punched platform ticket . . .

My Sad Face

While I was standing on the dock watching the seagulls, my sad face attracted the attention of a policeman on his rounds. I was completely absorbed in the sight of the hovering birds as they shot up and swooped down in a vain search for something edible: the harbour was deserted, the water greenish and thick with foul oil, and on its crusty film floated all kinds of discarded junk; not a vessel was to be seen, the cranes had rusted, the freight sheds collapsed; not even rats seemed to inhabit the black ruins along the wharf, silence reigned. It was years since all connection with the outside world had been cut off.

I had my eye on one particular seagull and was observing its flight. Uneasy as a swallow sensing thunder in the air, it usually stayed hovering just above the surface of the water, occasionally, with a shrill cry, risking an upward sweep to unite with its circling fellows. Had I been free to express a wish, I would have chosen a loaf of bread to feed to the gulls, crumbling it to pieces to provide a white fixed point for the random flutterings, to set a goal at which the birds could aim, to tauten this shrill flurry of crisscross hovering and circling by hurling a piece of bread into the mesh as if to pull together a bunch of strings. But I was as hungry as they were, and tired, yet happy in spite of my sadness because it felt good to be standing there, my hands in my pockets, watching the gulls and drinking in sadness.

Suddenly I felt an official hand on my shoulder, and a voice said: 'Come along now!' The hand tugged at my shoulder, trying to pull me round, but I did not budge, shook it off, and said quietly: 'You're nuts.'

'Comrade,' the still invisible one told me, 'I'm warning you.'

'Sir,' I retorted.

'What d'you mean, "Sir"?' he shouted angrily. 'We're all comrades.'

With that he stepped round beside me and looked at me, forcing me to bring back my contentedly roving gaze and direct it at his simple, honest face: he was as solemn as a buffalo that for twenty years has had nothing to eat but duty.

'On what grounds . . .' I began.

'Sufficient grounds,' he said. 'Your sad face.'

I laughed.

'Don't laugh!' His rage was genuine. I had first thought he was bored, with no unlicensed whore, no staggering sailor, no thief or fugitive to arrest, but now I saw he meant it: he intended to arrest me.

'Come along now!'

'Why?' I asked quietly.

Before I realized what was happening, I found my left wrist enclosed in a thin chain, and instantly I knew that once again I had had it. I turned towards the swerving gulls for a last look, glanced at the calm grey sky, and tried with a sudden twist to plunge into the water, for it seemed more desirable to drown alone in that scummy dishwater than to be strangled by the sergeants in a back yard or to be locked up again. But the policeman suddenly jerked me so close to him that all hope of wrenching myself free was gone.

'Why?' I asked again.

'There's a law that you have to be happy.'

'I am happy!' I cried.

'Your sad face . . .' he shook his head.

'But this law is new,' I told him.

'It's thirty-six hours old, and I'm sure you know that every law comes into force twenty-four hours after it has been proclaimed.'

'But I've never heard of it!'

'That won't save you. It was proclaimed yesterday, over all the loudspeakers, in all the papers, and anyone' – here he looked at me scornfully – 'anyone who doesn't share in the blessings of press or radio was informed by leaflets scattered from the air over every street in the country. So we'll soon find out where you've been spending the last thirty-six hours, Comrade.'

He dragged me away. For the first time I noticed that it was cold and I had no coat, for the first time I became really aware of my hunger growling at the entrance to my stomach, for the first time I realized that I was also dirty, unshaved, and in rags, and that there were laws demanding that every comrade be clean, shaved, happy, and well-fed. He pushed me in front of him like a scarecrow that has been found guilty of stealing and is compelled to abandon the place of its dreams at the edge of the field. The streets were empty, the police station was not far off, and, although I had known they would soon find a reason for arresting me, my heart was heavy, for he took me through the places of my childhood which I had intended to visit after looking at the harbour: public gardens that had been full of bushes, in glorious confusion, overgrown paths – all this was now levelled, orderly, neat, arranged in squares for the patriotic groups obliged to drill and march here on Mondays, Wednesdays, and Saturdays. Only the sky was as it used to be, the air the same as in the old days when my heart had been full of dreams.

Here and there as we walked along I saw the government sign displayed on the walls of a number of love-barracks, indicating whose turn it was to participate in these hygienic pleasures on Wednesdays; certain taverns also were evidently authorized to hang out the drinking sign, a beer glass cut out of tin and striped diagonally with the national colours: light brown, dark brown, light brown. Joy was doubtless already filling the hearts of those whose names appeared in the official list of Wednesday drinkers and who would thus partake of the Wednesday beer.

All the people we passed were stamped with the unmistakable mark of earnest zeal, encased in an aura of tireless activity probably intensified by the sight of the policeman. They all quickened their pace, assumed expressions of perfect devotion to duty, and the women coming out of the goods depots did their best to register that joy which was expected of them, for they were required to show joy and cheerful gaiety over the duties of the housewife, whose task it was to refresh the state worker every evening with a wholesome meal.

But all these people skilfuly avoided us in such a way that no one was forced to cross our path directly; where there were signs of life on the street, they disappeared twenty paces ahead of us, each trying to dash into a goods depot or vanish round a corner, and quite a few may have slipped into a strange house and waited nervously behind the door until the sound of our footsteps had died away.

Only once, just as we were crossing an intersection, we came face to face with an elderly man, I just caught a glimpse of his schoolteacher's badge. There was no time for him to avoid us, and he strove, after first saluting the policeman in the prescribed manner (by slapping his own head three times with the flat of his hand as a sign of total abasement) – he strove, as I say, to do his duty by spitting three times into my face and bestowing upon me the compulsory epithet of 'filthy traitor'. His aim was good, but the day had been hot, his throat must have been dry, for I received only a few tiny, rather ineffectual flecks which – contrary to regulations – I tried involuntarily to wipe away with my sleeve, whereupon the policeman kicked me in the backside and struck me with his fist in the small of my back, adding in a flat voice: 'Phase One,' meaning: first and mildest form of punishment administerable by every policeman.

The schoolteacher had hurriedly gone on his way. Everyone else managed to avoid us; except for just one woman who happened to be taking the prescribed stroll in the fresh air in front of a love-barracks prior to the evening's pleasures, a pale, puffy blonde who blew me a furtive kiss, and I smiled gratefully while the policeman tried to pretend he hadn't noticed. They are required to permit these women liberties that for any other comrade would unquestionably result in severe punishment; for, since they contribute substantially to the general working morale, they are tacitly considered to be outside the law, a concession whose far-reaching consequences have been branded as a sign of incipient liberalization by Prof. Bleigoeth, Ph.D., D.Litt., the political philosopher, in the obligatory periodical for (political) philosophy. I had read this the previous day on my way to the capital when, in a farm outhouse, I came across a few sheets of the magazine that a student – probably the farmer's son – had embellished with some very witty comments.

Fortunately we now reached the police station, for at that moment the sirens sounded, a sign that the streets were about to be flooded with thousands of people wearing expressions of restrained joy (it being required at closing time to show restraint in one's expression of joy, otherwise it might look as though work were a burden; whereas rejoicing was to prevail when work began – rejoicing and singing), and all these thousands would have been compelled to spit at me. However, the siren indicated ten minutes before closing time, every worker being required to devote ten minutes to a thorough washing of his person, in accordance with the motto of the head of state: Joy and Soap.

The entrance to the local police station, a squat concrete box, was guarded by two sentries who, as I passed them, gave me the benefit of the customary 'physical punitive measures', striking me hard across the temple with their rifles and cracking the muzzles of their pistols down on my collarbone, in accordance with the preamble to State Law No. 1: 'Every police officer is required, when confronted by any apprehended [meaning arrested] person, to demonstrate violence *per se*, with the exception of the officer performing the arrest, the latter being privileged to participate in the pleasure of carrying out the necessary physical punitive measures during the interrogation.' The actual State Law No. 1 runs as follows: 'Every police officer *may* punish anyone: he *must* punish anyone who has committed a crime. For all comrades there is no such thing as exemption from punishment, only the possibility of exemption from punishment.'

We now proceeded down a long bare corridor provided with a great many large windows; then a door opened automatically, the sentries having already announced our arrival, and in those days, when everything was joy, obedience, and order and every-one did his best to use up the mandatory pound of soap a day, in those days the arrival of an apprehended [arrested] comrade was naturally an event.

We entered an almost empty room containing nothing but a desk with a telephone and two chairs. I was required to remain standing in the middle of the room; the policeman took off his helmet and sat down.

At first there was silence, nothing happened. They always do it like that, that's the worst part. I could feel my face collapsing by degrees, I was tired and hungry, and by now even the last vestiges of that joy of sadness had vanished, for I knew I had had it.

After a few seconds a tall, pale-faced, silent man entered the room wearing the light-brown uniform of the preliminary in-terrogator. He sat down without a word and looked at me.

'Status?'

'Ordinary comrade.'

'Date of birth?'

'1.1.1.,' I said.

'Last occupation?'

'Convict.'

The two men exchanged glances.

'When and where discharged?'

'Yesterday, Building 12, Cell 13.'

'Where to?'

'The capital.'

'Certificate.'

I produced the discharge certificate from my pocket and handed it to him. He clipped it to the green card on which he had begun to enter my particulars.

'Your former crime?'

'Happy face.'

The two men exchanged glances.

'Explain,' said the interrogator.

'At that time,' I said, 'my happy face attracted the attention of a police officer on a day when general mourning had been decreed. It was the anniversary of the Leader's death.'

'Length of sentence?'

'Five.'

'Conduct?'

'Bad.'

'Reason?'

'Deficient in work-enthusiasm.'

'That's all.'

With that the preliminary interrogator rose, walked over to me, and neatly knocked out my three front centre teeth: a sign that I was to be branded as a lapsed criminal, an intensified measure I had not counted on. The preliminary interrogator then left the room, and a fat fellow in a dark-brown uniform came in: the interrogator.

I was beaten by all of them: by the interrogator, the chief interrogator, the supreme interrogator, the examiner, and the concluding examiner; in addition, the policeman carried out all the physical punitive measures demanded by law, and on account of my sad face they sentenced me to ten years, just as five years earlier they had sentenced me to five years on account of my happy face.

I must now try to make my face register nothing at all, if I can manage to survive the next ten years of Joy and Soap . . .

Candles for the Madonna

My stay here was a brief one; I had an appointment in the late afternoon with the representative of a firm that was toying with the idea of taking over a product which has been causing us something of a headache: candles. We put all our money into the manufacture of tremendous stocks on the assumption that the electricity shortage would continue indefinitely. We have worked very hard, been thrifty and honest, and when I say 'we' I mean my wife and myself. We are producers, wholesalers, retailers; we combine every stage in the holy estate of commerce: we are agents, workmen, travelling salesmen, manufacturers.

But we put our money on the wrong horse. There is not much demand for candles these days. Electricity rationing has been abolished, even most basements now have electric light again; and at the very moment when our hard work, our efforts, all our struggles, seemed about to bear fruit – the production of a large quantity of candles – at that precise moment the demand dried up.

Our attempts to do business with those religious enterprises dealing in what are known as devotional supplies came to nothing. These firms had hoarded candles in abundance – better ones than ours, incidentally, the fancy kind, with green, red, blue, and yellow ribbons, embroided with little golden stars, winding around them – like Aesculapius' snake – and enhancing both their reverent and aesthetic appeal; they also came in various lengths and sizes whereas ours are all identical and of simple design: about ten inches long, smooth, yellow, quite plain, their only asset the beauty of simplicity.

We were forced to admit that we had miscalculated; compared with the splendid products displayed by the devotional supply houses, our candles look humble indeed, and nobody buys anything humble-looking. Nor has our willingness to reduce our price resulted in any increase in sales. On the other hand, of course, we lack the money to plan new designs, let alone manufacture them, since the income we derive from the limited sale of the stock we have produced is barely enough to cover our living expenses and steadily mounting costs. I have, for instance, to make longer and longer trips in order to call on genuinely or apparently interested parties, I have to keep on reducing our price, and we know we have no alternative but to unload the substantial stocks still on our hands and find some other means of making a living.

I had come to this town in response to a letter from a wholesaler who had intimated that he would take a considerable quantity off my hands at an acceptable price. I was foolish enough to believe him, came all the way here, and was now calling on this fellow. He had a magnificent apartment, luxurious, spacious, furnished in great style, and the large office where he received me was crammed with samples of all the various products that make money for his type of business. Arranged on long shelves were plaster saints, statuettes of Joseph, Virgin Marys, bleeding Sacred Hearts, mild-eyed, fair-haired penitents whose plaster pedestals bore the name, in a variety of languages and embossed lettering (choice of gold or red): Madeleine, Maddalena, Magdalena, Magdalene; Nativity scenes (complete or sectional), oxen, asses, Infant Jesuses in wax or plaster, shepherds, and angels of all ages: tots, youths, children, greybeards; plaster palm leaves adorned with gold or silver Hallelujahs, holy-water stoups of stainless steel, plaster, copper, pottery: some in good taste, some in bad.

The man himself – a jovial, red-faced fellow – asked me to sit down, affected some initial interest, and offered me a cigar. He wanted to know how we happened to get into this particular branch of manufacturing, and after I had explained that we had inherited nothing from the war but a huge pile of stearin which my wife had salvaged from four blazing trucks in front of our bombed-out house and which no one had since claimed as their property, after I had smoked about a quarter of my cigar, he suddenly said, without any preamble: 'I'm sorry I had you come here, but I've changed my mind.' Perhaps my sudden loss of colour did strike him as odd after all. 'Yes,' he went on, 'I really am sorry about it, but after considering all the angles I've come to the conclusion that your product won't sell. It won't sell! Believe me, I know! Sorry!' He smiled, shrugged his shoulders, and held out his hand. I put down the half-smoked cigar and left.

By this time it was dark, and I was a total stranger in the town. Although, in spite of everything, I was aware of a certain relief, I had the terrible feeling that I was not only poor, deceived, the victim of a misguided idea, but also ridiculous. It would seem that I was unfit for the so-called battle of life, for the career of manufacturer and dealer. Our candles would not sell even for a pittance, they weren't good enough to hold their own in the field of devotionalist competition, and we probably wouldn't even be able to give them away, whereas other, inferior candles were being bought. I would never discover the secret of business success, although, with my wife, I had hit upon the secret of making candles.

I lugged my heavy sample case to the streetcar stop and waited a long time. The darkness was soft and clear, it was summer. Streetlights were on at the crossings, people were strolling about in the evening, it was quiet; I was standing beside a big circular traffic island – fringed by dark empty office buildings – behind me a little park; I heard the sound of running water, and on turning round I saw a great marble woman standing there, with thin jets of water spouting from her rigid breasts into a copper basin; I felt chilly and realized I was tired. At last the streetcar arrived; soft music poured from brightly lit cafés, but the station was in an empty, quiet part of town. All I could glean from the big blackboard there, was the departure time of a train which would get me only halfway home and which, if I took it, would cost me a whole night of waiting-room, grime, and a bowl of repulsive soup at the station in a little place with no hotel. I turned away, went outside again, and counted my money by the light of a gas lamp; nine marks, return ticket, and a few pfennigs. Some cars were standing there that looked as if they had been waiting there forever, and little trees, cropped like new recruits. Dear little trees, I thought, nice little trees, obedient little trees. Doctors' white nameplates showed up against a few unlighted houses, and through a café window I looked in on a gathering of empty chairs for whose benefit a writhing violinist was producing sobs that might have moved stones but hardly a human being. At last, in a lane skirting the bulk of a dark church, I came upon a painted green sign: 'Rooms.' I stepped inside.

Behind me I could hear the streetcar on its return trip to the better lighted, more populated part of town. The hall was empty, and I turned to the right into a little room containing four tables and twelve chairs; to the left, bottles of beer and lemonade stood in metal display stands on a built-in counter. Everything looked clean and plain. Green hessian, divided by narrow strips of brown wood, had been tacked to the walls with rosette-shaped copper nails. The chairs were green too, upholstered in some soft, velvety material. Light-yellow curtains had been drawn closely across the windows, and behind the counter a serving hatch opened into a kitchen. I put down my suitcase, drew a chair towards me, and sat down. I was very tired.

How quiet it was here, even quieter than the station which, strangely enough, was some distance from the business centre, a gloomy, cavernous place filled with the muffled sounds of an invisible bustle: bustle behind closed wickets, bustle behind wooden barriers.

I was hungry too, and I found the utter futility of this journey very depressing. I was glad of the few minutes to myself in this quiet, unpretentious room. I would have liked to smoke but found I had no cigarettes, and now I regretted having abandoned the cigar in the wholesale devotionalist's office. Although I might well be depressed at having gone on yet another wild-goose chase,

I was aware of a growing sense of relief that I couldn't quite define or account for, but perhaps in my heart I rejoiced at my final expulsion from the devotional-supply trade.

I had not been idle after the war; I had helped clear away ruins, remove rubble, scrape bricks clean, build walls, haul sand, shift lime, I had submitted applications – many, many applications – thumbed through books, carefully watched over my pile of stearin. On my own, with no help from those who might have given me the benefit of their experience, I had found out how to make candles, beautiful, simple, good-quality candles, tinted a soft yellow that gave them the lustre of melting beeswax. I had done everything to get on my feet, as they say: to find some way of earning a living, and although I ought to have been sad – the very futility of my efforts was now filling me with a joy such as I had never known.

I had not been ungenerous, I had given away candles to people living in cramped unlighted holes, and whenever there had been a chance of profiteering I had avoided it. I had gone hungry and devoted myself single-mindedly towards this method of making a living; but, although I might have expected a reward for what one might call my integrity, I almost rejoiced to find myself evidently unworthy of any reward.

The thought also crossed my mind: perhaps we would have done better after all to manufacture shoe polish, as someone had advised us, to mix other ingredients with the basic material, to get hold of some formulas, acquire a stock of cardboard containers, and fill them up.

In the midst of my musings the landlady entered the room, a slight, elderly woman. Her dress was green, the green of the beer and lemonade bottles on the counter. 'Good evening,' she said pleasantly. I returned her greeting, and she asked: 'What can I do for you?'

'I would like a room, if you have one.'

'Certainly,' she said, 'what price had you in mind?'

'The cheapest.'

'That would be three marks fifty.'

'Fine,' I said, relieved. 'And perhaps something to eat?'

'Certainly.'

'Bread, some cheese and butter, and . . .' I ran my eyes over the bottles on the counter, 'perhaps some wine.'

'Certainly,' she said, 'a bottle?'

'No, no! A glass and – how much will that come to?'

She had gone behind the counter and was already pushing back the hook to open the serving hatch, but she paused to ask: 'Altogether?'

'Yes please, altogether.'

She reached under the counter, took out pad and pencil, and again it was very quiet while she slowly wrote and added up. Despite the reserve in her manner, her whole presence, as she stood there, radiated a reassuring kindness. And she endeared herself to me still further by apparently making several mistakes in her addition. She slowly wrote down the items, frowned as she added them up, shook her head, crossed them out, rewrote everything, added up again, this time without frowning, and in grey pencil wrote the result at the bottom, finally saying in her soft voice: 'Six-twenty – no, six, I beg your pardon.'

I smiled. 'That's fine. And have you any cigars?'

'Certainly.' She reached under the counter again and held out a box. I took two and thanked her. The woman quietly gave the order through to the kitchen and left the room.

Scarcely had she gone when the door opened and in walked a young man, of slight build, unshaven, wearing a light-coloured raincoat; behind him was a girl in a brown coat, hatless. The couple approached quietly, almost diffidently, and with a brief 'Good evening' turned towards the counter. The boy was carrying the girl's shabby leather holdall, and although he was obviously at pains to appear undaunted and to display the bravado of a man who regularly spends the night with his girl in a hotel, I could see his lower lip trembling and tiny beads of sweat on the stubble of his beard. The couple stood there like customers awaiting their turn in a store. The fact that they were hatless and that the holdall was their only luggage made them look like refugees who had arrived at some transit camp. The girl was beautiful, her skin alive, warm, and slightly flushed, and her heavy brown hair hanging loosely over her shoulders seemed almost too heavy for her slender feet; she nervously moved her black dusty shoes, shifting her weight from one foot to the other more often than was necessary; the young man kept brushing back a few strands of hair as they fell over his forehead, and his small round mouth expressed a painful but at the same time elated determination. I could see they were deliberately avoiding each other's eyes, and they did not speak to one another, while I for my part was glad to be busily occupied with my cigar, to be able to clip it, light it, look critically at the tip, relight it, and start smoking. Every second of waiting must be agony, I knew; for the girl, no matter how unabashed and happy she might look, continued to shift her weight as she tugged at her coat, while the boy continued to pass his hand over his forehead although there were no more strands of hair to brush back. At last the woman reappeared, quietly said 'Good evening,' and placed the bottle of wine on the counter.

I jumped up at once, saying: 'Allow me!' She looked at me in surprise, then set down the glass, handed me the corkscrew, and asked the young man: 'What can I do for you?' As I put the cigar between my lips and twisted the corkscrew into the cork, I heard the young man ask: 'Can you let us have two rooms?'

'Two?' asked the landlady: just then I pulled out the cork and from the corner of my eye saw the girl flush, while the boy bit hard on his lower lip and, barely opening his mouth, said: 'Yes, two.' 'Oh, thank you,' the landlady said, filling the glass and passing it to me. I went back to my table, began to sip the gentle wine, and could only hope that the inevitable ritual would not be dragged out even further by the arrival of my supper. But the entries of the register, the filling out of forms, and the producing of grey-blue identity cards, all took less time than I had expected; and at one point, when the boy opened the hold-all to get out the identity cards, I saw that it contained greasy paper bags, a crumpled hat, some packets of cigarettes, a beret, and a shabby old red wallet.

During all this time the girl tried to look poised and confident; with an air of nonchalance she surveyed the bottles of lemonade, the green of the hessian wall-covering, and the rosette-shaped nails, but the flush never left her cheeks, and when everything was finally settled they took their keys and hurried upstairs without saying good night. A few minutes later my supper was passed through the hatch; the landlady brought me my plate, and when our eyes met she did not smile, as I had thought she would, but looked gravely past me and said: 'I hope you enjoy your supper, sir.'

'Thank you,' I replied. She remained standing beside me.

I slowly began my meal, helping myself to bread, butter, and cheese. She still did not move. 'Smile,' I said.

And she did smile, but then she sighed, saying: 'There's nothing I can do about it.'

'Do you wish there were?'

'Oh yes,' she said fervently, sitting herself down beside me, 'indeed I do. I'd like to do something about a lot of things. But if he asks for two rooms . . . If he had asked for one, now . . .' she paused.

'What then?' I asked.

'What then?' she mimicked angrily, 'I would have thrown him out.'

'What for?' I said wearily, putting the last piece of bread in my mouth. She said nothing. What for, I thought, what for? Doesn't the world belong to lovers, weren't the nights mild enough, weren't other doors open, dirtier ones perhaps, but doors one could close behind one? I looked into my empty glass and smiled . . .

The landlady had risen, fetched her big book and a pile of forms, and sat down beside me again.

She watched me as I filled everything out. I paused at the column 'Occupation', raised my eyes, and looked into her smiling face. 'Why do you hesitate?' she asked calmly, 'have you no occupation?'

'I don't know.'

'You don't know?'

'I don't know whether I am a workman, a salesman, a manufacturer, unemployed, or only an agent . . . but whose agent . . .' whereupon I quickly wrote down 'Agent' and gave her back the book. For a moment I considered offering her candles – twenty, if she liked, for a glass of wine, or ten for a cigar. I don't know why I didn't, perhaps I was just too tired, or too lazy, but the next morning I was glad I hadn't. I relighted my dead cigar and got to my feet. The woman had shut the book, laying the forms between the pages, and was yawning.

'Would you like coffee in the morning?' she asked.

'No thank you, I have to catch an early train. Good night.'

'Good night,' she said.

But next morning I slept late. The passage, which I had glimpsed the previous evening – carpeted in dark red – had remained silent throughout the night. The room was quiet too. The unaccustomed wine had made me sleepy but also happy. The window was open, and all I could see against the quiet, deep-blue summer sky was the dark roof of the church opposite; further to the right I could see the colourful reflection of the town lights, hear the noise of the livelier district. I took my cigar with me as I got into bed so that I could read the newspaper, but fell asleep at once . . .

It was after eight when I woke up. The train I had meant to catch had already left, and I was sorry I had not asked to be woken. I washed, decided to go out for a shave, and went downstairs. The little green room was now light and cheerful, the sun shining in through the thin curtains, and I was surprised to see tables laid for breakfast, with breadcrumbs, empty jam dishes, and coffee-pots. I had felt as if I were the only guest in this silent house. I paid my bill to a friendly maid and left.

Outside I hesitated. The cool shadow of the church surrounded me. The lane was narrow and clean; to the right a baker had opened his shop, loaves and rolls shone pale brown and yellow in the glass cases, and further on jugs of milk stood at a door to which a thin, blue-white trail of milk drops led. The other side of the street was entirely taken up by a high black wall built of great square blocks of stone; through a big arched gateway I saw green lawn and walked in. I was standing in a monastery garden. An old, flat-roofed building, its stone window frames touchingly whitewashed, stood in the middle of a green lawn; stone tombs in the shade of weeping willows. A monk was padding along a flagged path towards the church. In passing, he gave me a nod of greeting, I nodded back, and when he entered the church I followed him, without knowing why.

The church was empty. It was old, devoid of decoration, and when by force of habit I dipped my hand in the stoup and bent my knee toward the altar, I saw that the candles must have just gone out: a thin, black ribbon of smoke was rising from them into the clear air. There was no one in sight; mass seemed to be over for this morning. My eyes involuntarily followed the black figure as it bobbed an awkward genuflection in front of the tabernacle and vanished into a side aisle. I went closer and came to a sudden halt: I found myself looking at a confessional, the young girl of the previous evening was kneeling in a pew in front of it, her face hidden in her hands, while at the edge of the nave, showing no apparent interest, stood the young man, the holdall in one hand, the other hanging slackly by his side, his eyes on the altar . . .

In the midst of this silence I could hear my heart beating, louder, stronger, strangely unquiet, and I could feel the boy looking at me: our eyes met, he recognized me, and flushed. The girl was still kneeling there, her face in her hands, a thin, faint thread of smoke was still rising from the candles. I sat down in a pew, placed my hat beside me, and put my suitcase on the ground. I felt as if I were waking up for the first time, as if until now I had seen everything with my eyes only, a detached spectator – church, garden, street, girl, man – it had all been like a stage set that I had brushed by as an outsider, but now, looking at the altar, I longed for the young man to go and confess too. I wondered when I had last gone to confession, found it hard to keep track of the years, roughly it would be about seven, but as I went on thinking about it I realized something much worse: I couldn't put my finger on any sin. No matter how honestly I tried, I couldn't think of any sin worth confessing, and this made me very sad. I felt unclean, full of things that needed to be washed away, but nowhere was there actually anything that in coarse, rough, sharp, clear terms could have been called sin. My heart beat louder than ever. Last night I had not envied the young couple, but now I did envy that ardent kneeling figure, still hiding her face in her hands, waiting. The young man stood completely motionless and detached.

I was like a pail of water that has remained exposed to the air for a long time. It looks clean, a casual glance reveals nothing in it: nobody has thrown stones, dirt, or garbage into it, it has been standing in the hallway or basement of a well-kept, respectable house; the bottom appears to be immaculate; all is clear and still, yet, when you dip your hand into the water, there runs through your fingers an intangible repulsive fine dirt that seems to be without shape, without form, almost without dimension. You just know it is there. And on reaching deeper into this immaculate pail, you find at the bottom a thick indisputable layer of this fine disgusting formless muck to which you cannot put a name; a dense, leaden sediment made up of these infinitesimal particles of dirt abstracted from the air of respectability.

I could not pray, I could only hear my heart beating and wait for the girl to go into the confessional. At last she raised her hands, laid her face against them for an instant, stood up, and entered the wooden box.

The young man kept his place. He stood there aloof, having no part in it, unshaven, pale, his face still expressing a mild yet insistent determination. When the girl emerged, he suddenly put down the holdall and stepped into the confessional.

I still could not pray, no voice spoke to me or in me, nothing moved, only my heart was beating, and I could not curb my impatience: I stood up, left my suitcase where it was, and crossed over to the side aisle, where I stood beside a pew. In the front pew the young woman was kneeling before an old stone Madonna standing on a bare, disused altar. The Virgin's face was coarse-featured but smiling, a piece of her nose was missing, the blue paint of her robe had flaked off, and the gold stars on it were now no more than lighter spots; her sceptre was broken, and of the Child in her arms only the back of the head and part of the feet were still visible. The centre part, the torso, had fallen out, and she was smilingly holding this fragment in her arms. A poor monastic order, evidently, that owned this church.

'Oh, if I could only pray!' I prayed. I felt hard, useless, unclean, unrepentant, I couldn't even produce one sin, the only thing I possessed was my pounding heart and the knowledge that I was unclean . . .

The young man brushing past me from behind roused me from my thoughts, and I stepped into the confessional . . .

By the time I had been dismissed with the sign of the cross, the young couple had left the church. The monk pushed aside the purple curtain of the confessional, opened the little door, and padded slowly past me; once again he genuflected awkwardly before the altar.

I waited until I had seen him disappear, then quickly crossed the nave, also genuflecting, carried my suitcase back to the side aisle, and opened it: there they all lay, tied in bundles by my wife's loving hands, slim, yellow, unadorned, and I looked at the cold, bare stone plinth on which the Madonna stood and regretted for the first time that my suitcase was not heavier. I ripped open the first bundle and struck a match . . .

Warming each candle in the flame of another, I stuck them all firmly onto the cold plinth that quickly allowed the soft wax to harden; on they all went, until the whole surface was covered with restless flickering lights and my suitcase was empty. I left it where it was, seized my hat, genuflected once more, and left: it was as if I were running away.

And now at last, as I walked slowly towards the station, I recalled all my sins, and my heart was lighter than it had been for a long time . . .

Black Sheep

It would seem that I have been singled out to ensure that the chain of black sheep is not broken in my generation. Somebody has to be the black sheep, and it happens to be me. Nobody would ever have thought it of me, but there it is: I am the one. Wise members of our family maintain that Uncle Otto's influence on me was not good. Uncle Otto was the black sheep of the previous generation, and my godfather. It had to be somebody, and he was the one. Needless to say, he was chosen as my godfather before it became apparent that he would come to a bad end; and it was the same with me – I became godfather to a little boy who, ever since I have been regarded as black, is being kept at a safe distance from me by his anxious family. As a matter of fact, they ought to be grateful to us, for a family without a black sheep is not a typical family.

My friendship with Uncle Otto began at an early age. He used to visit us often, bringing more candies than my father thought good for us, and he would talk and talk until he finally ended up cadging a loan.

Uncle Otto knew what he was talking about. There was not a subject in which he was not well-versed: sociology, literature, music, architecture, anything at all – and he knew his subject, he really did. Even specialists in their field enjoyed talking to him; they found him stimulating, intelligent, an uncommonly nice fellow, until the shock of the attendant attempt to cadge a loan sobered them up. For that was the outrageous thing about it: he did not confine his marauding to the members of the family but laid his artful traps wherever a favourable prospect seemed to present itself.

Everyone used to say he could 'cash in' on his knowledge – as the older generation put it – but he didn't cash in on it, he cashed in on the nerves of his relatives.

He alone knew the secret of managing to give the impression that on this particular day he would not do it. But he did do it. Regularly, relentlessly. I fancy he could not bring himself to pass up an opportunity. His conversation was so fascinating, so full of genuine enthusiasm, clearly conceived, brilliantly witty, devastating for his opponents, uplifting for his friends: he could converse far too well on any topic for anyone to have dreamed that he would . . .! But he did. He knew all about infant-care, although he had never had any children, he would involve young mothers in irresistibly fascinating discussions on diet for this or that ailment, suggest types of baby powder, write out ointment prescriptions, decide the quantity and quality of what they were given to drink, he even knew how to hold them: a squalling infant, when put into his arms, would quiet down immediately. He radiated a kind of magic. And he was equally at home analysing Beethoven's Ninth Symphony, composing legal opinions, citing from memory some law that happened to be under discussion . . .

But, regardless of time and topic, as the conversation approached its end and the moment of parting drew inexorably nearer – usually in the entrance hall with the front door already half-shut – he would thrust his pale face with its lively dark eyes once more through the door and, right into the apprehension of the tensely waiting relatives, remark quite casually to the head of that particular family: 'By the way, I wonder if you could . . .?'

The amounts he demanded fluctuated between one mark and fifty marks. Fifty was the uppermost limit: over the decades it had become an unwritten law that he was never to ask for more. 'Just to tide me over!' he would add. To tide him over – this was his favourite phrase. He would then come in again, replace his hat on the hall stand, unwind his muffler, and launch into an explanation of why he needed the money. He always had plans, infallible plans. He never needed it directly for himself: its sole purpose was to place his livelihood at last on a firm footing. His plans varied from a soft-drink stand, which he was confident would yield a regular steady income, to the founding of a political party which would preserve Europe from its decline and fall.

The words 'By the way, I wonder if you could . . .' were apt, as the years went by, to scare the wits out of our family; there were wives, aunts, great-aunts, even nieces, whom the sound of 'just tide me over' would bring to the verge of fainting.

Uncle Otto – I assume him to have been in the best of humours as he sprinted down the stairs – then took himself off to the nearest bar to mull over his plans. He would mull over them to the tune of one schnapps or three bottles of wine, depending on the size of the loan he had been able to raise.

I will no longer conceal the fact that he drank. He drank, yet no one had ever seen him drunk. Moreover, he evidently felt a need to drink alone. To offer him alcohol in the hope of dodging the request for a loan was so much wasted effort. An entire barrel of wine would not have deterred him, at the very last minute, when he was on the point of leaving, from thrusting his head once more through the door and asking: 'By the way, I wonder if you could – just to tide me over . . .?'

But his worst trait I have so far kept to myself: sometimes he would repay a loan. Every so often he appeared to earn money in one way or another: as a former law student he occasionally, I believe, dispensed legal advice. At such times he would turn up, take a bill from his pocket, smooth it out with wistful tenderness, and say: 'You were kind enough to help me out – here are your five marks!' Whereupon he would leave very quickly and return after a maximum of two days to ask for a sum slightly in excess of the one he had repaid. He alone knew the secret of managing to reach the age of almost sixty without ever having what is commonly called a regular occupation. Nor was his death in any way due to some illness he might have contracted as a result of his drinking. He was as fit as a fiddle, his heart was perfectly sound, and he slept like a healthy innocent babe full of his mother's milk that sleeps away the hours till the next meal.

No, he died very suddenly: he lost his life in an accident, and what happened after his death remains the greatest mystery of all.

Uncle Otto, as I say, was killed in an accident. He was run over by a truck and trailer in heavy downtown traffic, and luckily it was an honest man who picked him up, called the police, and notified the family. In his pockets they found a wallet containing a medallion of the Virgin Mary, a weekly pass good for two more streetcar rides, and twenty-four thousand marks in cash plus the carbon copy of a receipt he had had to sign for the lottery bureau, and he cannot have been in possession of the money for more than a minute, probably less, because the truck ran over him scarcely fifty yards from the lottery bureau. What followed was rather humiliating for the family. His room bore the stamp of poverty: table, chair, bed, and closet, a few books, and a large notebook, and in this notebook an accurate list of all those to whom he owed money, including an entry for a loan that had brought him in four marks the previous evening. Also a very brief will naming me his heir.

As his executor it was my father's job to pay the outstanding debts. Indeed, Uncle Otto's list of creditors filled an entire quarto-sized notebook, his first entry going back to the years when he had suddenly broken off his legal career to devote himself to other plans, the mulling over of which had cost him so much time and so much money. His debts totalled nearly fifteen thousand marks, the number of his creditors over seven hundred, ranging from a streetcar conductor who had advanced him thirty pfennigs for a transfer, to my father, who had altogether two thousand marks coming to him, probably because Uncle Otto had always found him such a soft touch.

Strangely enough, I happened to come of age on the very day of the funeral and was therefore entitled to enter upon my inheritance of ten thousand marks, so I immediately broke off my university career to devote myself to other plans. In spite of my parents' tears, I left home to move into Uncle Otto's room. It held a great attraction for me, and I am still living there although my hair is now no longer as thick as it used to be. The contents of the room have neither increased nor decreased. Today I know that I made many mistakes in those early years. It was ridiculous to attempt to become a musician, let alone a composer, I have no talents in that direction. Today I know this, but I paid for the knowledge with three years of useless study and the inevitability of acquiring a reputation for loafing, besides which it used up my whole inheritance, but that's a long time ago.

I have forgotten the sequence of my plans, there were too many of them. Besides, the periods of time needed for me to recognize their futility became shorter and shorter. I finally reached the point where one plan managed to last just three days, a life span that even for a plan is too short. The life span of my plans dwindled so rapidly that they eventually became mere lightning flashes of ideas that I could not explain to anyone because they were not clear even to me. When I think that I devoted myself for three whole months to the science of physiognomy until I finally decided in the course of a single afternoon to become a painter, a gardener, a mechanic, and a sailor, and that I fell asleep thinking I was born to be a teacher and woke up firmly convinced that a career in the customs service was what I was cut out for . . . !

In short, I had neither Uncle Otto's charm nor his relatively great endurance. I am not a talker either: I sit silent among other people, I bore them and blurt out my attempts to extract money from them so abruptly into the silence that they sound like extortions. Only with children do I get along well, this is at least one favourable attribute that I seem to have inherited from Uncle Otto. Babies quiet down the minute I take them in my arms, and when they look at me they smile, insofar as they can smile at all, although it is said that my face scares people. Unkind people have advised me to found the profession of male kindergarten teacher as its first exponent and to put an end to my eternal planning by bringing at least this plan to fruition. But I never shall. I think this is what makes us so impossible: the fact that we cannot cash in on our real talents – or, to adopt the modern jargon: exploit them financially.

One thing is certain, though: if I am a black sheep – and personally I am by no means convinced of this – but if I am one, it is of a different kind from Uncle Otto. I lack his light touch, his charm; besides, my debts weigh heavily on me, while obviously his scarcely bothered him at all. And I did a terrible thing: I capitulated – I asked for a job. I implored the family to help me, to find me a job, to pull strings for me, so that for once, just once, I might be assured of tangible compensation in return for the performance of clearly defined duties. And they were successful. After I had sent off my petitions, given written and verbal form to my pleas, my urgent, imploring appeals, I was horrified to find they had been taken seriously and borne fruit, and I did something which no black sheep had ever done before: I did not flinch, did not turn it down, I accepted the position they had managed to find for me. I sacrificed something that I ought never to have sacrificed: my freedom!

Each evening when I came home I could have kicked myself for letting yet another day of my life go by that had brought me nothing but fatigue, rage, and just enough money to enable me to keep on working, if one can call what I was doing work: sorting bills alphabetically, punching holes in them, and fastening them into a brand-new file where they patiently submitted to the fate of never being paid; or writing the kind of circulars that travel ineffectually out into the world and amount to nothing but a superfluous burden for the mailman; and sometimes making out bills that now and then were actually paid in cash. I had to deal with salesmen who strove in vain to palm off the rubbish manufactured by our boss. Our boss: that bustling blockhead who is forever in a hurry and never does a thing, who persistently chatters away the precious hours of the day – an existence of stultifying stupidity – who never dares admit the extent of his debts, who cheats his way from one bluff to the next, a balloon-artist who starts blowing up one balloon the very moment another one bursts, leaving behind a repulsive rubber rag that a second earlier still had sheen, life, and bounce.

Our office was right alongside the factory, where a staff of a dozen or so manufactured the kind of furniture that, once bought, is an annoyance for the rest of one's life unless one decides after three days to chop it up into kindling: occasional tables, sewing cabinets, midget chests of drawers, arty little 'hand-painted' chairs that collapse under the weight of three-year-old children, little stands for vases or flowerpots, shoddy bric-à-brac that ostensibly owes its existence to the art of the cabinet-maker whereas in fact an inferior workman, using cheap paint purporting to be enamel, produces a semblance of attractiveness intended to justify the prices.

So this was how I spent my days, one after another – nearly two weeks in all – in the office of this unintelligent man who not only took himself seriously but considered himself an artist, for now and again – it happened only once while I was there – he was to be seen standing at the drawing-board, shuffling pencils and paper and designing some wobbly object or other, a flower stand or a new portable bar, yet another source of annoyance for future generations.

The appalling futility of his devices never seemed to enter his head. When he had finished designing one of these gadgets – as I say, it happened only once while I was working for him – he would dash off in his car to rest up from his creative labours, a respite that lasted a week after he had worked for only fifteen minutes. The drawing was tossed in front of the foreman, who would spread it out on his bench, study it with furrowed brow, and proceed to check the lumber supplies in order to get production under way. For days I could watch the new creations piling up behind the dusty windows of the workshop – he called it a factory: wall shelves or radio stands that were hardly worth the glue being wasted on them.

The only objects of any use were those turned out by the workmen without the boss's knowledge, when they could be quite certain of his absence for a few days: little stools or jewel cases of pleasing sturdiness and simplicity – great-grandchildren will straddle them or hoard their treasures in them; sensible laundry racks on which the shirts of many a future generation will flutter. What was endearing and serviceable was thus produced illegally.

But the really memorable personality I came across during this interlude of business life was the streetcar conductor who invalidated each day for me with his punch. He would take the slip of paper, my weekly pass, push it into the open maw of his punch, and an invisible supply of ink would blot out half an inch of it – one day out of my life, one precious day that had brought me nothing but fatigue, rage, and just enough money to continue in this futile pursuit. A godlike authority was vested in this man wearing the unpretentious uniform of the city transit system, the man who evening after evening wielded sufficient power to declare thousands of human days null and void.

To this day I feel annoyed with myself for not giving notice before I was practically forced to give notice; for not telling the boss where to get off before I was practically forced to tell him: but one day my landlady brought a sinister-looking individual along to my office who introduced himself as a lottery-bureau operator and announced that I was now the owner of a fortune of fifty thousand marks, provided that I was such and such a person and that I was the holder of a certain lottery ticket. Well, I was such and such a person and I was the holder of the lottery ticket. I quit my job on the spot, without giving notice, taking it upon myself to abandon the bills unpunched, unsorted, and there was nothing left for me to do but go home, collect the cash, and by way of money orders acquaint my relatives with the new state of affairs.

It was evidently expected of me to die soon or become the victim of an accident. But for the time being no automobile appears to have been singled out to deprive me of my life, and my heart is as sound as a bell although I do not spurn the bottle. So after paying my debts, I find myself the possessor of a fortune of nearly thirty thousand marks, tax free, and a sought after uncle who has suddenly regained access to his godchild. But then children love me anyway, as I have said, and now I am allowed to play with them, buy them balls, ice cream, sundaes, I am allowed to buy whole gigantic clusters of balloons, and to populate the roundabouts and swings with the merry little throng.

While my sister has promptly bought her son, my godchild, a lottery ticket, I now spend my time wondering, musing for hours, about who among this new generation is going to be my successor; which of these thriving, romping, lovely children begotten by brothers and sisters will be the black sheep of the next generation? For we are a typical family, and always will be. Who will be a good boy up to that point at which he ceases to be a good boy? Who will suddenly wish to devote himself to other plans, infallible, better plans? I would like to know, I would like to warn him, for we too have learned by experience, our calling also has its rules of the game which I could pass on to him, my successor, still unknown, still playing with the gang like a wolf in sheep's clothing . . .

But I have a foreboding that I shan't live long enough to recognize him and initiate him into our secrets. He will come forward, reveal his true colours, when I die and it is his turn to take over. With flushed cheeks he will confront his parents and tell them he is fed up; and secretly I can only hope that when that time comes there will still be some of my money left, because I have changed my will and left the balance of my fortune to the one who shows the first incontrovertible signs of being earmarked as my successor . . .

The main thing is that he shouldn't let them down.

MORE ABOUT PENGUINS, PELICANS AND PUFFINS

For further information about books available from Penguins please write to Dept EP, Penguin Books Ltd, Harmondsworth, Middlesex UB7 ODA.

In the U.S.A.: For a complete list of books available from Penguins in the United States write to Dept DG, Penguin Books, 299 Murray Hill Parkway, East Rutherford, New Jersey 07073.

In Canada: For a complete list of books available from Penguins in Canada write to Penguin Books Canada Ltd, 2801 John Street, Markham, Ontario L3R 1B4.

In Australia: For a complete list of books available from Penguins in Australia write to the Marketing Department, Penguin Books Australia Ltd, P.O. Box 257, Ringwood, Victoria 3134.

In New Zealand: For a complete list of books available from Penguins in New Zealand write to the Marketing Department, Penguin Books (N.Z.) Ltd, P.O. Box 4019, Auckland 10.

In India: For a complete list of books available from Penguins in India write to Penguin Overseas Ltd, 706 Eros Apartments, 56 Nehru Place, New Delhi 110019.

VLADIMIR NABOKOV IN PENGUINS

THE GIFT

Life and memory, tradition and heritage all intertwine in the shimmering tapestry of the writer's mind.

Fyodor Godunov-Cherdynstev is an impoverished writer living in Berlin after the First World War, and it is through him that we see art and life converge: his childhood in Russia, recaptured in a volume entitled 'Poems'; Pushkin entering his blood, and with Pushkin's voice merges the voice of his father; while all the time Zina's vibrant presence continues to influence his work. As Nabokov unfolds his phantasmal tale, the threads gather together to foreshadow the book Fyodor dreams of writing: *The Gift.*

LOLITA

'Massive, unflagging, moral, exquisitely shaped, enormously vital, enormously funny' – Bernard Levin

Nabokov's novel of a middle-aged Englishman's passion for a honey-hued, twelve-year-old American girl, has become one of the world's great love stories.

'No lover has thought of his beloved with so much tenderness, no woman has been so charmingly evoked, in such grace and delicacy, as Lolita' – Lionel Trilling

and

A RUSSIAN BEAUTY
ADA
BEND SINISTER
DESPAIR
GLORY
INVITATION TO A
   BEHEADING
LAUGHTER IN THE DARK
LOOK AT THE HARLEQUINS!

NABOKOV'S DOZEN
PALE FIRE
PNIN
SPEAK, MEMORY:
   AN AUTOBIOGRAPHY
THE REAL LIFE OF
   SEBASTIAN KNIGHT
TYRANTS DESTROYED

SAUL BELLOW IN PENGUINS

HERZOG

'A well-nigh faultless novel' – *New Yorker*
'Clearly a major work of our time' – *Guardian*
Herzog is alone, now that Madeleine has left him for his best
friend. Solitary, in a crumbling old house which he shares with
the rats, he is buffeted by a whirlwind of mental activity.
People rumoured that his mind had collapsed. Was it true?

THE ADVENTURES OF AUGIE MARCH

From Saul Bellow here is another BIG book: the rumbustious,
larger-than-life adventures of Augie March spawned in Chicago,
torpedoed from the Merchant Marine, apprenticed to the
'International Set', ex-poker-player *extraordinaire*. Augie
March is the all-time once-met-never-forgotten American. He
discovers the world – and himself – with all the brashness and
gusto of a modern Columbus.

and

DANGLING MAN
THE DEAN'S DECEMBER
HENDERSON THE RAIN KING
HUMBOLDT'S GIFT
MR SAMMLER'S PLANET
MOSBY'S MEMOIRS AND OTHER STORIES
SEIZE THE DAY
TO JERUSALEM AND BACK
THE VICTIM

JORGE LUIS BORGES IN PENGUINS

LABYRINTHS

The twenty-three stories in *Labyrinths* include Borges's classic 'Tlön, Uqbar, Orbis Tertius', a new world where external objects are whatever each person wants; and 'Pierre Menard', the story of the man who rewrote parts of *Don Quixote* for the twentieth century in Cervantes's words.

The ten essays reflect the extraordinary scope of Borges's reading – the ancient literatures of Greece and China, the medieval philosophers, Pascal, Shakespeare, Valéry, Shaw and Wells – while the seven parables are unforgettable exercises in the art of astonishment.

THE BOOK OF SAND

'These superb new stories ... make marvellous thought-provoking reading ... Borges ponders, questions, examines time, reality, thought, in extraordinary fashion in these haunting, seemingly simple, very beautiful stories. A major literary event' – *Publishers Weekly*

This volume also contains *The Gold of the Tigers: Selected Later Poems*, in which understatement replaces some of the glittering fireworks of Borges's poetry.

and

THE BOOK OF IMAGINARY BEINGS
DOCTOR BRODIE'S REPORT
A UNIVERSAL HISTORY OF INFAMY

HEINRICH BÖLL IN PENGUINS

AND NEVER SAID A WORD

The spare and sensitive account of a marriage.

Fred and Käte live apart. Oppressed by the responsibility of feeding his five children and by family life in a single room, Fred has left, to drift round a strange half-world of cafés and bars.

Käte is the strength of the family, but when she discovers she is expecting their sixth child it seems that the news can only push the couple further apart. Yet it is this shock that finally allows Fred to accept his position.

In a novel that ends on a remarkable note of tranquillity and hope, Nobel-Prize winner Heinrich Böll displays his remarkable perception of human relationships.

GROUP PORTRAIT WITH LADY

'It conveys, with concreteness and vitality, the detailed quality of ordinary life in the Hitler years and at the time of their catastrophic end' – *Sunday Telegraph*

'Leni (the central character) is seen through a series of interviews with witnesses who make up this huge 'group portrait'. This works brilliantly as a parody of fashionable documentary; then by making the story resonant with overlapping echoes; and finally by counterpointing these voices of the imagination with the terrible dead language of real documents of Nazi bureaucracy' – *Guardian*

'A work of considerable distinction' – *The Time Literary Supplement*

and

AND WHERE WERE YOU, ADAM?

THE BREAD OF THOSE EARLY YEARS

THE END OF A MISSION

THE LOST HONOUR OF KATHARINA BLUM

THE TRAIN WAS ON TIME